ADORE YOU

NICOLE FALLS

D1715854

Silent N Publishing

DEDICATION

To Pee Wee, may you never read this :)

ACKNOWLEDGMENTS

It's been a long road. I feel like I've been writing a book nearly as long as I've been reading books, ha! But I've finally made it by the grace of God. There have been tons of people who have been instrumental in the genesis of this finally coming to fruition, so to all of you who have listened to me lament about this book, I thank you. Your never-ending patience will not go unrewarded. And now for some special shoutouts...

Mama: Thank you for support & an unwavering faith in your lastborn.

Daddy: Thank you for an undying pledge to ensure that I doggedly pursue my heart's desires at all costs.

Ajua: Nineteen, my Leo sister. Thank you for being consistent with check-ins & reminding me of our brilliance.

Ashley: You'll never know how the words "So. I love your story." filled my heart with so much glee. Thank you for being an awesome beta reader & friend.

Christina: This book wouldn't be here without you, full stop. I'm eternally grateful for your friendship & at a complete loss with where to even begin to repay you for the incredible amounts of patience, kindness & advice you've bestowed upon me. #HeadJonesie4Life

Dom: Forever grateful for your friendship, patience, candidness, and feedback. [insert Mary gif here]

Kayla: Your undying support of my all of writing has never gone unnoticed & I cannot begin to tell you how much it means to me. Remember I told you whenever I finally finished a book; you'd be in my acknowledgements. See, I wasn't lying!

Sarah: Thank you for keeping me on task & delivering a swift kick to my ass every time I tried to quit & just being an all around dope ass friend.

Tahmeka: A few years ago you started a writing group & were it not for that group; this book would still be a figment floating in the ether of my imagination. Thank you for being the catalyst, my friend!

Tawanda: The bio assist was clutch. You the real MVP.

Trina: My sis, my ace...thank you for caring about these crazy folks from my brain and asking intermittently what the hell ever happened with them. Hope I managed to keep your attention, ha!

And finally to the readers, I hope you enjoyed reading this one and will keep rockin' with ya girl as I keep on keepin' on.

1

DEVORAH

I wandered down to the lobby bar of my hotel in search of...well that was yet to be determined. I just knew that this staycation needed to consist of more than me prancing around in a fluffy bathrobe, singing Beyoncé tunes at the top of my lungs as I danced around my room. So I moisturized, fixed my face, slid into a sundress and took the elevator down to WXYZ. Walking across the lobby into the bar area, I had immediate second thoughts. What I was hoping would be a low-key hotel lobby bar was actually popping. Luckily for me there was exactly one stool left at the bar. I walked over and snagged it before some girl who looked like a newborn calf walking could reach it. I raised a hand in the air to grab the attention of a bartender.

"Double Makers...rocks," I said over the music playing.

The bartender looked at me sympathetically and said, "Let me upgrade your bourbon. Please."

"Or you could just bring me what the fuck I ordered," I countered with a slight smirk.

"Feisty! I like it! Aight bet...I'll make you a deal. You

try my bourbon suggestion. If you don't like it better than Maker's Mark, I'll gladly cover your tab for the night. Deal?"

I knew there had to be a catch to this. Either he was stupidly overconfident or his suggestion was going to be damn good bourbon. However it shook out, I'd win because bourbon. He looked at me expectantly, extending a hand to shake on the deal. *What the hell,* I thought, sliding my palm into his.

"Deal."

The bartender moved about five feet away, grabbing an oblong shaped bottle with a label I couldn't read from my perch. He pulled a rocks glass from below the bar and put an ice sphere inside. He then poured two very generous jiggers worth of this mystery bourbon into the glass before returning to stand in front of me.

"Cherry?" he asked.

I just held out my hand for the drink expectantly. I took a sip and tried with all my might not to show the pleasure that coursed through me as soon as the slightly cooled amber liquid hit my lips. My eyes closed of their own volition as the oaky flavor hit the back of my tongue. Before I knew it, a slight shiver overtook my body as I swallowed. *Goddamn, that was smooth*.

"Well?" the bartender asked with one eyebrow raised.

"It's aight..." I said, fighting to sound casual.

I was also fighting to keep a satisfied smile off of my face. That one sip made the hundreds of gallons of Maker's I'd undoubtedly consumed in the past ten years taste like somebody's grandpappy's moonshine. The bartender's eyes twinkled knowingly, so I was sure my physical reaction hadn't gone unnoticed by him.

"Oh it's more than aight. I saw that shimmy. This

smooth jazz that is playin' ain't coercing any moves like that outta you."

"Ok, so you know your shit."

"That's some mouth you got on you."

"Problem?" I huffed, agitated.

"Not at all."

A man approached to my left and signaled to the bartender.

"I'll be back. You let me know if you need anything else."

The bartender walked away to serve the guy and I took a good look at him. I was in such a mood that I initially didn't notice how handsome he was. He looked to be at least six feet tall with skin the color of mahogany. The crisp, white button down he wore, with sleeves rolled up to the elbow, showcased a body that was clearly no stranger to the gym. Broad shoulders and well-defined pecs that tapered down into what I was certain were abs that would make me weep. That body, combined with a smile that was surely the product of orthodontia, had me thinking things I certainly should not have been thinking. I shook off the salacious thoughts about the barkeep and continued sipping my bourbon. Lusting after this guy who was clearly too young for me was not in the plan for these few days of staycation. And I certainly didn't need the stress of another man in my life giving me grief. The one I was currently avoiding was more than enough.

Hell, truthfully *he* was one of the reasons that I needed to get away. Dealing with catching unexpected feelings when this was just supposed to be a mutual satisfaction of needs was not in the game plan. Couple that with the fact that I had been stressed at work and I needed this little respite. So I decided that a stay at a boutique hotel in the

City would be the cure. I planned a few days of spa treatments, decadent food, and drinks. It would be capped off with seeing my darling babyniece Sophie in her dance recital on Saturday afternoon. As soon as we'd wrapped the Hartman Enterprises project, I booked my stay at the hotel. I didn't even travel back home to the burbs to pack a bag, instead choosing to splurge and buy a couple new outfits and necessities to get me through the next few days.

"So what's your story?" the bartender grinned as he came back over to me.

I let my eyes travel up his body slowly, while sipping my drink.

"Really? How cliché?" I laughed.

"So what brings you here tonight? You're too fine to be sitting here by yourself."

"Who says I'm by myself? I could be meeting someone."

"You're too relaxed to be meeting someone. You've been at my bar for fifteen minutes without a second glance to your phone. In fact, it's been face down on the bar this entire time as if you're avoiding it..."

Score one for Mr. Bartender and his keen observation skills. I *was* avoiding the phone. As if it knew we were talking about it, my phone vibrated at that moment. I was reluctant to even look at it. Releasing a sigh, I turned my phone over to look at the text I'd just received.

Call me. - Cadence

Of course it was Cade. She had tried to contact me no less than fifty times since I told her that I was staying in the City for a little R&R. We talked briefly right before I'd checked into the hotel before I came up with an excuse to ring off the line. I tapped out a reply and sat my phone back down, face up this time. Almost immediately, it rang. The bartender had been looking on in amusement this entire time.

"Hold my seat?" I asked and then rushed off to a quieter place to answer the phone without waiting for his answer.

"Yes, mom?"

"Har de har, bitch. You wish this was your mom."

"Cadence Melody McPherson, I told you I was fine!"

"And you also told me you were drinking bourbon in a hotel lobby bar. Which..."

"It's gin that makes you sin, not bourbon. I'm fine, Cade...really."

And I was. For once my mind was clear; the only thoughts swimming around in my head were finding out the name of the bartender's mystery bourbon and whether or not I wanted steak for dinner.

"Ok, girl. So have you decided to talk—"

"We're not talking about Voldemort, Cade, remember?"

"You came up with that silly ass rule; not me. You need to just be real with—"

"Lalalalala..." I began singing off key into the phone. Childish, but it was a sure fire tactic to shut my best friend up as she went on a rant that I could probably quote verbatim now.

"Fine. I'll drop it...*for now*. I just...go find your bliss, friend. Please. You deserve it more than anyone I know."

"This is my bliss, Cade. Total relaxation and bourbon being served to me by a man more handsome than he needs to be. I couldn't ask for anything more."

Except I could ask for a whole lot more. Namely, companionship. That was the one area in my life that always seemed to be lacking, no matter how hard I tried. Without fail, I was either in a drought with no available prospects or the object of my desire was inappropriate. We were in the season of the latter, currently.

"You know I just worry about you."

"I know, mom."

"Speaking of mom...you're not the only one who'll be calling me that soon."

"I'm sorry, come again? Are you really telling me that you're pregnant via the phone?"

"Yes. Because your trifling ass refused all six of my pleas for you to come see me prior to your staycation."

"I thought you'd want to talk about—"

"That's what you get for assuming..." Cadence trailed off.

"Oh my goodness, I'm so fucking happy for you and Geoff! You're gonna be a mama, Cade!" I sighed.

Cadence and Geoff had been trying for a few years, but she hadn't been able to get pregnant. I was so overjoyed at the fact that her biggest dream was finally coming true. Cadence was going to be a great mom and I was ever grateful to be the babysitting, baby spoiling auntie once again.

"You could have this too, if you'd just—"

"Bye, Cade."

I hung up the phone, walked back toward WXYZ and my handsome bourbon provider. I slid onto the stool once again, poised to order a new drink, but he must have been watching and saw my return. I didn't even need to signal him as I saw him walking toward me with a fresh glass of bourbon.

"You're smiling now. I take it that call brought good news?"

"It did."

"So now can you tell me what someone as fine as you is doing here alone?"

"There you go assuming again. Who said I was alone?"

"Touché."

The bartender sauntered away to take care of another customer as my phone buzzed. I picked it up; noticing that there were three new text messages.

I need to see you. - E

Cadence says you're at the Aloft. I'm on my way. - E

Have a Macallan neat waiting. - E

Shit. Meddling best friends who don't know how to leave your life alone were the fucking worst. I signaled to the bartender.

"Ready for another already?" he asked with a slight lift of his brow.

The glass he'd poured mere minutes ago was still full.

I heaved a sigh and asked, "Do you have Macallan?"

———

I came awake, slowly, in an unfamiliar bed. My mouth felt like I'd spent the night playing the chubby bunny game — dry, yet sticky. An arm was slung low on my waist, pulling me into the hard line of a body whose identity I was afraid to know. The last thing I remembered from last night was bourbon. And lots of it. Whoever was behind me shifted in his sleep and pulled me closer. I felt his chin dig into my shoulder as he pressed a kiss into my neck and murmured something I could barely understand. I was on high alert, wracking my brain about who it could be. His voice was muffled since he'd spoken directly into my skin, so I couldn't readily place it. Whoever he was had my height dwarfed by at least a foot if the legs stretching way past where mine ended were any indication. I felt the hardness of his erection coming to life, pressing into the small of my back, growing larger as he awakened. I didn't want to turn around, so I shifted slightly to rustle the sheet so I could at least see the arm clutching me so tightly. A downward glance showed me a milk chocolate colored arm. *Sooooo...it's not the bartender. Shit.*

"Good morning, Bee," the voice murmured, kissing my shoulder.

Mr. Chocolate's identity was now crystal clear. The events of the previous night flooded my mind and I was slow to extricate myself from his embrace. I allowed myself to forget everything else and just be.

I exhaled slowly and said, "You shouldn't be here, El..."

"But, I am...and you love it," Ellis paused, kissing a path from my shoulder to my ear. Hands that were as busy as his mouth traveled up my torso, making their way to my breasts, which he palmed firmly.

Involuntarily, a moan escaped my mouth as he tweaked my nipple. He wasn't playing fair; he knew that I was putty in his hands and powerless to resist once he'd started. I turned in his embrace, throwing a leg over his hip as I angled my head up for a kiss. Ellis lowered his head slowly, lips hovering dangerously close to mine, but not making contact.

I closed the incremental distance between our mouths with a swipe of my tongue across his lips. That drew a low grumble from him; so I repeated the action until he took over the kiss. Ellis eased me onto my back as his tongue slid between my lips to tangle with mine. The kiss was unhurried, as our tongues parried for dominance. His hands traveled down my body, settling in a grip on my thighs. He ran a single finger along the outside of each thigh; a feather light touch that he knew would immediately make me crave more. It was a move he called *the open sesame*. Against my will, my legs parted wider for him to trail those same fingers along my inner thighs.

"You don't play fair," I moaned.

Ellis just kept his fingers moving until he reached his destination. Zeroing in on my clit with his thumb, he asked "You still ready for me to go?"

He didn't give me a chance to respond before pressing down and circling once, causing me to spread even wider for him. He slipped a finger inside, stroking my wetness. His mouth went back to my breasts, nipping and suckling until both nipples hardened into peaks. *Dammit now he really wasn't playing fair.* He dipped another finger inside of me, moving both in a come hither motion, while his thumb was still pressing and rotating against my clit. My hips began to roll in sync with his strokes.

"Mmmmmmm..."

"What's that now?" he asked, sliding his fingers out slowly and replacing them with his dick.

Instead of slamming into me like I was accustomed, Ellis slid in slowly, breaking down any shred of resistance I had left. My eyes fluttered closed as I moved with the slow strokes Ellis doled out. I felt myself getting closer to spiraling out of control when Ellis suddenly stopped. I opened my eyes to see him just staring at me, as if in a trance. I ran my hands up his spine, to pull him closer.

"Hi," I said.

Ellis shook his head quickly and leaned down to kiss me once again, still not moving.

"Hey."

"You need a break or somethin' because..."

Ellis smirked slightly. He eased my right leg up to wrap around his waist, moved back to adjust the angle and slammed into me. He repeated that action three more times, each time drawing out a bit more slowly and slamming into me a bit harder. The last time he plunged in deep, grinding his hips against mine; the base of his shaft coming into direct contact with my clit. That movement instantly sent me over the edge, moaning my way into release. Ellis kept stroking me through to another orgasm as he growled into his own. Shifting so that he didn't crush me under his weight, but still keeping us intimately connected, Ellis maneuvered us onto our sides as we both fought to regain control of our breathing. His fingers trailing up and down my spine didn't do much to calm the aftershocks that still wracked my body.

The euphoria I felt after orgasm faded quickly as I realized we'd done it again. I wasn't supposed to be back in this place with Ellis, but something kept drawing me back. And not only had we done it again, but we'd done it without protection. Thank God for my IUD. The last thing I needed from we were doing was a damn kid. Or shit truthfully, an STD. Cadence assured me that I was the only one El was body bumpin' with, but until I heard those words from his mouth I couldn't be certain. There was only so much you're privy to as the closest female friend of a man. Couple that with her also being my best friend and her insights into how he was really moving were limited at best.

Ellis would be the perfect man if he were not the brother of the ex everyone thought I would eventually marry. We all grew up together—me, Ellis, Everett and Cadence. Cade, Ev and I were the same age and El was three years older. Our mothers were sorority line sisters, so whenever they got together, we got together. Cadence and I literally grew up together, living in the same neighborhood, while our interactions with the guys were less frequent since they lived about an hour away in the suburbs. Somewhere along the way our "brothers" became unrequited objects of our affection. Well, my affection anyway. Cade didn't give a rat's ass about either of the Taylor brothers. It was Everett, however, that I ended up dating from junior year of high school through the first semester of our freshman year of college. Much of that was through the machinations of our mothers, desperate to unite our families in some way.

Dating Everett was just comfortable. He was my best friend outside of Cadence, so I always felt safe with him. I wasn't getting any play from anyone at my school, Ev had always been handsome and our mothers blessed the union, so I figured why not! We never had any sort of spark though, but our platonic love was so deep I was convinced that sparks were just figments of my imagination. At least that's what I thought until Ev met Cassidy and sparks immediately flew. Cass was one of my suite mates at Hunt Valley State University, which I attended for undergrad. It was, coincidentally, where Ellis was finishing up his undergraduate career by the time I arrived on campus. Everett and I decided to go different universities; he had a full ride for a state school and the graphic design program – my major – at Hunt Valley was one of the best in our state. So we traded off weekends visiting one another. The first few weekends that he came to visit me at HVSU, Cass wasn't there. Everett had met all of my other suite mates, but he and Cass were like two ships passing in the night. Until one weekend when those ships' paths aligned.

You know how they say it's uncomfortable to be in a room with unrestrained tension. Well, imagine being in a room with barely restrained passion. From the first introduction, I could tell that Everett was attracted to Cassidy. When they shook hands he held on a little too long, staring into her eyes as if he were dazed. I chalked it up to the typical male response to Cassidy that I had grown used to rather quickly. Cass was strikingly beautiful – a half Irish, half Black American beauty with skin that was the color of café au lait, piercing emerald eyes, and shockingly red kinky curls, corkscrewing in every direction. When I first met her, I had major hair envy and thought for sure I would not get along with her at all. It turned out that besides being ridiculously good-looking she was the most down-to-earth person I would meet in my time at HVSU. We clicked instantaneously, forging a lifelong friendship.

We spent a lot of time with Cass that weekend she and Everett finally met and it almost felt like I was encroaching on their budding relationship at moments. They had the same nerdy sense of humor, so they'd be laughing at jokes one or the other cracked that went right over my head. Initially I was jealous until I sat in the living room watching them laughing hysterically at an episode of some geeky television show and it hit me. Later that night as we lay in my bed, I asked Everett his impressions of Cass.

He got that same moony look in his eye from when they were introduced and replied, "She's chill. I like her. Yeah. She's good people."

"Oh yeah, I could tell you liked her," I replied, my voice holding a note of amusement.

Hearing the shift in my tone, Everett rushed to assure

me that he just thought she was a nice person, but I stopped him in the middle of his explanation.

"I think we should break up, Ev."

"What? Where is this coming from, Devorah?"

"Hold my hand."

I slid my fingers down his arm to clasp his so that we were holding hands, palm to palm.

"What do you feel?"

"I feel your clammy ass hand, holding onto mine for dear life. Quit playing, Bee."

I smiled upon hearing him use my childhood nickname. After finding out my name meant bee as an eight year old, I became obsessed with all things bee related. As a result, Ellis started calling me Little Bee. Eventually Cade and Everett joined in too and the name stuck.

"What else?"

"What do you mean what else? Nothing. I just feel you holding my hand."

"Exactly. That's my point, Ev."

"Huh? What are you talki—"

I interrupted, "Now what did you feel when you shook Cass' hand this morning?"

"I-I di-didn't fe-feel—"

"You still stammer when you lie, huh?"

As kids, Ellis clued Cade and me into Everett's tendency to stutter when he was stretching the truth. The fact that he knew that we knew and still was unable to control it was amusing to say the least.

"Hear me out. I know you felt something because *I* felt something watching y'all interact all day. It wasn't jealousy or even anger. It was as if blinders had been lifted. I love you, Ev. I truly, truly do, but I'm not sure that I'm in love with you. And something in my shundo is telling me that you feel the same about me. But seeing you with Cassidy, witnessing that spark? That's something that is undeniable. There's chemistry there, but here? There is only familiarity."

"Bee...you trippin'. I don't even know her like that."

"But I know both of you well enough to know that this is something I need to do. You just have to trust me. Matter of fact, I'll be right back..."

I got out of bed and knocked on Cass' bedroom door. After speaking with her about the same suspicions I'd shared with Everett, I dragged her into my room. Ev was still sitting on my bed looking like a deer in headlights when Cass and I returned.

"Y'all talk. I'ma be in Cass' room. Come get me when you come to your senses."

I wound up sleeping in Cass' room that night. Those fools were up all night connecting and have basically been inseparable since. I was Best Honorable Maiden at their wedding; a bastardized portmanteau of Best Man and Maid of Honor because I was the one who brought them together. My mother was still a bit pissed that I "gave Everett to that redheaded lil girl" and brought it up whenever she lamented about my single status or still not having grandkids. I was sure my mother would have a field day with...whatever this was I was doing with Ellis. And by field day, I meant be completely mortified. She wanted grandbabies, but I was certain she didn't want them by way of me being involved with two of her best friend's sons.

This never would have happened if my boss hadn't sent me to that damn conference. Wouldn't have found myself in one of the most romantic cities in the states with a man I'd pined after for an embarrassingly long time. Wouldn't have agreed to take that moonlight stroll that ended with my ankles knocking against his ears. Wouldn't have had the most delicious orgasms I've had in my life and been permanently ruined for every other man who dared try.

"Uh oh...what's that look about, Bee?"

"You know we—"

"I know I know. We shouldn't have done this. Scandal. Shame. Fire and brimstone. All that shit," Ellis droned with an amused look on his face.

"This isn't funny, El. And this really is the last time." I tried to sound resolute.

"You said that last time, but still somehow ended up bent over my balcony as I slid into..."

Involuntarily, a shudder wracked my body. That day was a true test of my flexibility. Who knew my leg could extend that far behind me?

"Stop. That's how this shit happens every time. I try to stop this, you distract me and then I end up with your dick in me," I pouted.

"Bee," Ellis said in a low rumble, "you do realize that you're not exactly proving your case with me still inside you, right?"

He moved to extract himself and I felt an immediate loss.

Heaving a sigh, I said, "Can you imagine what Imogene and Miranda would say if they saw us right now?"

"Really, Bee? Well, you've definitely managed to kill any arousal left by mentioning my mother and Aunt Im. But I'm sure after they got over the shock of seeing us naked as the day we were born; they'd have no problems. Because we're adults with free will..."

Ellis had given me at least twenty versions of this speech each time I tried to end our relationship. Well, I shouldn't even say end a relationship because there wasn't anything to end. We just had an undeniable chemistry and the absolute best sex of my life. Those two things did not a relationship make. Not for lack of trying on Ellis' part though. He'd been sweating me to define what we were doing since we got back from New Orleans. But who wanted to be known as the girl who dated two brothers? Childish, I was fully aware, but there were other things holding me back. Ellis hadn't exactly been known to be one-woman man. And I mean...after spending the majority of my life wanting him and finally getting some of him, how devastated would I be once I lost him? Of course none of this was shit I could share with him.

2

ELLIS

I was getting really fucking tired of having the same conversation with Devorah. Since this thing between us started she'd been really weird about whatever this was that was unfolding. I certainly didn't expect to run into her at that conference, let alone end the night, falling asleep embedded inside her, but here we were. Honestly though? This shit was inevitable. I'd wanted her for some time now. When she ended up at Hunt Valley, I probably shouldn't have been lusting after my little brother's girl, but damn, milk definitely did Little Bee's body good. By the time she stepped foot on campus, she had grown out of her gangly teen years into a fine ass woman. She'd always carried herself gracefully, the byproduct of years of being a dancer, but that scrawny frame morphed into curves in all the right places—a fat ass and titties that would make a man weep. Combine that with her heart shaped face, wide doe-like eyes and a full mouth and I was a goner.

I should have never listened to Cadence and come down here, but I couldn't help it. Never had any woman ever fucked me up like this. Sweating her best friend to track her down on some stalker shit? Not even your boy's style; yet here we were. I should have stuck with the whole element of surprise thing, but when I showed up Devorah didn't seem as put out as I would have expected. I thought she was softening to the idea of whatever this was becoming official, but clearly not.

"Why do you want me?" Devorah's voice broke into my thoughts. "Why are you pressing the issue so hard? I mean...look at you. You can get pussy on demand, I'm sure."

Smirking, I reached over and pushed her hair back from covering her eyes. She shuddered at the simple touch. I couldn't lie; I was just as affected whenever we touched. I didn't know what the hell this was, but this thing between us was electric. And I was intrigued.

"That's why," I said, simply, "How many times have we done this in the past six months? And every time I touch you, something as simple as tucking your bangs, you have a strong reaction. I've never felt any shit like this, Bee. So I wanted to see what it's all about."

She shifted her gaze from mine to stare at something over my shoulder. That break in eye contact meant the conversation was over. Apparently my honest answer wasn't good enough. I swear this woman captivated and drove me insane at the very same time.

"You want me to go?" I asked, not really wanting to move a damn inch.

"You shouldn't even be here."

"That's not what I asked though..."

She was saved from answering by my phone ringing. Who in the hell...*ah shit*!

"What up, E?"

"What up? Nigga, I'm inside your house ready to go hoop and you are...where, exactly?"

I hesitated briefly before saying, "I had to make a run. Gimme forty-five and I'll meet you at the court."

"Make a run, huh? Which one of the hoes is it this time? Aye if it's shorty who does the tongue thing? I'll give you an hour, bro," Everett laughed.

I couldn't help the chuckle that escaped.

"Aye, man. Chill. It ain't like that."

"So what exactly is it like then?" Everett asked, laughing.

"Mind your business, ET."

"Wouldn't have to if your ass was at home like you supposed to be."

"Aight. Chill. Damn. Just told you I'd be there in forty-five."

"Man, you might as well take the whole hour. I'll be here soaking up your good AC and eating what's in your... aw nigga you ain't even got no groceries?"

"Get out of my house and meet me at Pembroke in an hour," I laughed.

"Yeah whatever, man. Got me out here when I coulda been still laid up with my wife."

"You shoulda called before you came. I'll see you soon. Bye."

I shook my head as I pressed the button to disconnect the call. Devorah had gotten out of bed and was in the shower singing off key to Beyoncé, typical morning after behavior. I walked into the bathroom to let her know I was leaving. I pulled back the shower curtain and goddamn it if I didn't want to call Ev back and tell him we'd hoop another day.

"Did you need something?" Devorah asked, a hint of annoyance in her voice.

I pulled my gaze from her soapy breasts and met her eyes. I was surprised to see them rimmed in red, as if she'd just recently finished crying. Quickly averting her gaze, she looked down busying herself with soaping her loofah sponge. I stripped immediately, stepped into the shower and pulled her into my arms, with little resistance. She still was looking down though, refusing to make eye contact. I tipped her chin up, forcing her to look at me. Her eyes were filled with tears, precariously balanced, ready to fall.

"Hey, are we good?"

"Don't recall inviting you to share my shower."

"You have a really annoying habit of not answering my questions."

"Does shorty who does that tongue thing answer your questions?"

Shit. I didn't realize she could hear that. Goddamn that Everett and his loud ass mouth. She pulled out of my embrace and tilted her head under the spray of the shower head. With her eyes closed, she let the water cascade over her face and hair.

"Bee, you know..."

Stepping from beneath the spray, Devorah said, "I don't know shit, Ellis."

I scrubbed a hand over my face and reached out to grab her hands.

"Look at me."

She turned her gaze to me, with water spiked eyelashes.

"I, Ellis Stacey Taylor the Third, do solemnly swear that I am not fucking anyone other than Devorah Nicole Lee when she feels like not being ornery."

"Your middle name is Stacey?"

"Yeah, it's a family name. Wait—damnit, how long have we known each other and you don't know my middle name? Really, Bee?"

"It never came up?" she giggled.

I pulled her flush against my body.

"Stop trying to derail. Do you understand what I just said?"

She looked down and nodded.

"And?"

Moments passed before she angled her head up, giving me a soft kiss wrought with sweetness. As she pulled away, she whispered, "I guess I gotta give up my hoes, huh?"

We both burst into laughter and she relaxed into my embrace. Crisis averted for now, hopefully. I would, however, have to talk to Everett about knowing when to shut the fuck up though. I lingered a bit longer, sharing Bee's shower before I headed out to my house and changed into gear to beat my brother's ass at basketball.

————

An hour later, I pulled up to Pembroke Park and saw Everett warming up.

"Bout time you got here, fool," he yelled out.

"Just be thankful I gave your ass extra practice time."

We played a few games of one-on-one before ceding the court to some teens that came to play five-on-five. As we headed back to our cars, Everett reminded me of his daughter Sophie's dance recital tomorrow afternoon. I confirmed I'd be there. On the ride home I decided to call my boy Trey to see if he wanted to watch the game. It was a ruse mainly because I needed someone to talk this Bee shit out with. Couldn't do it with my brother since she was being all crazy about the family knowing, so my next closest friend would do. I pressed the voice activated command button on my steering wheel.

Please say a command after the tone.

"Call Trey Ball."

Calling Trey Ball iPhone.

"ET! What up, dude? Long time..."

"Shit. What's good with you, boy?"

"Not a damn thing besides Demetria driving me insane..."

"Aw shit you havin' girl troubles, too?"

"Too?"

Shit. I didn't mean to drop that in there so early.

"What you got goin' on today? Game tonight. Come through, let's crack some brews; talk some shit."

"Talk about that 'too'."

"Man, I was just..."

"Cut the shit, bruh. I'll be there by six with brews and ears to hear all about Ms. Me Too," Trey laughed.

"Aight, man. I'll catch you later."

"Later."

As promised, Trey showed up with brews at six on the dot. I swear he was the most punctual brother I knew. CP time didn't fly when he was around. It was a side effect of his upbringing as a Marine brat. His pops didn't play that being late shit at all. We managed to break most of his goody two shoes tendencies in undergrad, but the timeliness stuck. I had ordered a pizza and it arrived shortly after Trey did. We watched the first half of the game talking shit about our squad's inability to get a single shot from beyond the arc to drop before he finally asked, "So who is Ms. Me Too?"

"I thought we were talking about your shit with Demi."

"Nah man, that's the same old marriage bullshit. I don't see why she just can't be content with what we got going on. Fifteen damn years and I ain't fucked nobody else, but she needs a white dress and party to confirm our love?"

"You just said you ain't goin' nowhere. Why not give in? Make your life that much easier."

"It's the principle..."

"Your principle is stupid. And you're just gonna end up driving Demi away eventually."

"Hmph. She's been here this long. She ain't going anywhere."

"Yeah, ok. Don't get too comfortable. Women are wild, unpredictable creatures. Just when you think you got 'em figured out they come and put some hoodoo on your ass."

"Ain't this some shit. Coming from you, the King of I'm Not Settlingville. Ms. Me Too got you thinking bout a ring?"

"Nah, man it ain't even like that."

"But it's like something for you to be over here pushing me toward marriage. You're the last one I thought would ever encourage that shit."

"You remember Little Bee?"

"Everett's old bad ass shorty? Of course. I could never forget an ass like that."

"That's Ms. Me Too."

"Bruh."

"Yeah..."

"Bruhhhhhhhh," Trey put his head down, chuckling, "How did *that* happen?"

"You remember when I went to AdTech six months ago? She was there. One thing led to another and..."

"BRUH."

"Will you stop fucking saying bruh?"

"I ain't got shit else to say, man. I didn't know you were into sloppy seconds," Trey laughed.

"Man, please. That girl has always been mine. Ain't no seconds."

"The hell you mean always been yours?"

"Just what I said."

I knew that when we were kids that Devorah had a little crush on me. I thought it was annoying when she used to follow me around. Then the summer after my first year of undergrad changed everything. Auntie Im needed some help around the house after her and Uncle James split, so my mom had Everett and I trade off going over to help mow the lawn, fix leaky sinks, shit like that. Whenever it was my turn, Bee always seemed to be underfoot, offering lemonade on scorching summer days when I was mowing the lawn or hot chocolate on wintry days while I shoveled and salted.

During that time, we'd talked a lot, gotten fairly close. Fast forward to a year later when I found out she and Everett were dating. Not gonna lie, that shit stung at first, but I knew she was always going to be mine and would be back eventually. I didn't sweat it too hard because I wasn't ready for her then, but I was more than ready now.

"So what's the deal? You met your match? She ain't falling for the Black Clooney charm?" Trey laughed and took a sip of his beer.

"This one is different, man. She might be...the unicorn princess."

Trey looked over at me as he struggled to keep the beer in his mouth.

"Aye man, you spit that shit out, you cleaning it up."

"The UP, my guy? You said she'd never exist."

The UP or unicorn princess was some shit I'd made up in undergrad when Trey and I roomed together. He kept a running commentary on all of the baddies I brought through our room and how one day one of 'em was gonna bring me to my knees. I told him she'd have to be a damn unicorn princess because no way in hell a woman was going to make me fall. We laughed hard over that and references to the UP had been plentiful throughout the rest of our friendship. A time or two I got caught up in the sweetness of a woman, but none of them were ever worthy of the UP title. So Trey knew I was serious.

"Bee's the UP."

"Does she know she's the UP?"

"Trey, she doesn't even know the UP origin story."

"*She doesn't even know the origin story* face ass. Nigga, that ain't what I asked. Have you *shown* her she's the UP?"

"She ain't giving me much of a chance. Hell I can barely pin her down to keep whatever we have going on now holding on."

"You gotta woo the shit outta her. None of that corny shit either. Because from what I remember Little Bee wasn't with the shits."

"She still ain't, bruh," I said, feeling my face break open into a grin, unprovoked.

Trey just looked at me in amazement. "Nigga, are you grinning? She got you wide open like that?"

"Aye, you remember the shit I gave you when you first came home talkin' nonstop about Demi after meeting the girl for just fifteen minutes? If you knew what I was thinking right now, you'd be getting me back, tenfold. But fuck the woo."

"Fuck the woo?"

"Yeah, man. Bee *ain't with the shits* as you so eloquently stated, so I got to craft a whole new way to come at her. All my regular tricks are dead in the water."

"So what are you gonna do?"

"Man, I haven't got the slightest clue. But I do have the ear of her best friend, so I gotta use that shit to my advantage."

"So what's ET got to say about this?"

"Not a damn thing because he doesn't know. In fact, you're the only one besides Cadence that knows."

"Wait. She's the UP and you're keeping shit on the hush? What part of the game is this?"

"Ain't my doing. She's freaking out about the family knowing, so I'm abiding by her wishes...for now. I'm just about sick of this shit though."

"So what you gonna do about it besides whine about it to me?"

"Ain't nobody whining, fool. Going to have to force her hand eventually. I know one thing for sure, we're too old to be sneaking around hoping our mamas don't find out we're dating."

"So you *are* thinking about settling down."

"I'm mean I'm not tryna run to the altar or nothin', but..."

I picked up my beer and took a long sip while staring at the TV. The game was boring as hell since we were losing, but there was nothing else to say. I had to think long and hard about what I had to do to make Devorah realize that this was something worth exploring. Hell, we both were too damn old to be playing games. And I knew both of our mothers would be thrilled to see us finally in real relationships. Since Everett, Bee had dated casually, but no one had been able to lock her down long term.

Most of the dudes she brought around to gatherings were cornballs who were not deserving of even being in her presence, honestly. The last clown that she brought around showed up to a barbecue in a damn tweed blazer with the patches on the elbows. Everett and I clowned the hell out of her about dude. Even Cade joined in. He didn't even make it from the Memorial Day barbecue to the 4th of July. I knew, thanks to Cadence, that she felt like none of the dudes she dealt with in the past had some shit she called The Zing...whatever that was.

Trey left shortly after the game ended when Demi called. From the sounds of the yelling I heard, that brother was definitely in for a long, rough night. I thought I heard her crying too, which meant Demi had been drinking. Tough as nails eighty percent of the time, but when she had a little too much to drink, she became an emotional mess. My boy needed to man up and give the woman what she wanted, honestly. And I needed to figure out what my woman needed and give it to her.

———

"Uncle Elllllllll!" I heard my niece screeching my name before I saw her mane of curly red hair and arms flailing about.

My car wouldn't start this morning, so I had been running bit late for the recital thanks to Uber. I ended up not being able to find a seat near the rest of the family once I arrived, however. Luckily, I arrived just in time to see Sophie's solo. I would have never heard the last of it from her if I had missed it. I wouldn't even have been able to fake it because somehow my seven year old niece had eagle eyed vision and made sure she accounted for every family member's whereabouts as she crossed the stage prancing, twirling and dancing. I'd never forget the time she called out Everett for yawning during one of her earliest performances. I walked over to join Soph and the rest of the family as they fawned over her. As I made my way through the group greeting everyone with hugs, daps, and kisses, I noticed one very important face missing.

"I asked you a question, Uncle El?" Sophie said, impatiently with a hand on her hip.

"I'm sorry Sweetpea, what'd you say?"

"Did you like it? I worked really hard and mommy and me practiced every day. And Mrs. Hampton? She said my part was real important because all of the rest of the girls had to follow me and even though I messed up a little bit everybody still followed though. So what did you think?"

I reached down, gathering Sophia in my arms to give her a kiss on the forehead. "It was great, Sweetpea. You danced to my favorite song and everything."

"Your favorite song is 'Who Run the World', Uncle El? You're so strange."

"You've got that right, baby girl. He sure is strange," a slightly throaty voice replied to Sophie's observation.

"Auntie Beeeebeeeee!" Sophie scrambled out of my arms and rushed over to Devorah.

"Beanie!" Devorah squealed in a voice that rivaled Sophie's.

I'd bet that it hadn't been more than a few days since they'd seen each other, but from their reactions you'd think it had been weeks. Hell you also woulda thought Bee was the one related by blood by the way Soph quickly deserted me for her. As they embraced and began their little secret handshake I took the time to shamelessly ogle Devorah. She'd let her hair revert back to its natural state and it was pulled up into a curly puff on the top of her head. With a face free from makeup and a ponytail, she looked much younger than her thirty-one years. Seeing the easy way she and Soph interacted made me visualize her interacting with our daughter. Bee had always been nurturing with what seemed like never ending patience, even when we were kids; so I knew that would no doubt translate into her being a great mother.

"Hello? Earth to Ellis? Do you read me?" Everett said, waving his hands in front of my face.

I was so caught up in my fantasy that I'd missed everyone hustling out of the building so we could go to Easy Like Sundae Morning for Sophie's requisite post-recital ice cream.

"Hey, man, can I roll with y'all to Easy Sundae?" I asked Everett as we exited the recital hall. "The whip is acting up, so I had to Uber it over here this morning."

"We full, bro. Mama, Pops, and the in-laws carpooled with us."

"Ah shit. Aight, tell Soph I'll come by later and take her for a special treat," I said, pulling out my phone to request an Uber home.

"Aye, Devorah," Everett called out, "You coming to Easy Like Sundae Morning?"

"Heck yeah. In fact, Beanie is riding with me."

"You got room for one more? Ellis' car is outta commission and he needs a lift."

Devorah briefly hesitated before answering. "Sure."

I flashed a brief grin before walking in her direction.

"Well, well, well, we seem to keep finding ourselves thrown together don't we, Little Bee?"

3

DEVORAH

"Soooooooo…?" Cadence looked at me expectantly.

I remained stone-faced, features locked into a grimace.

"You can't not talk to me forever, Bee, so cut the shit. You agreed to this brunch date so you can't be that upset."

"I agreed to come because this is my favorite restaurant and you're paying. But fuck you. You're still not off the hook."

Cadence called yesterday and asked me to meet her at Cluck for brunch. She knew I was powerless to resist the combo of two of my favorite things, fried chicken and bottomless mimosas, so I was at her mercy. I didn't, however, have to make nice. I was still pissed at her for dropping the dime to Ellis about where I was at during my staycation. She was supposed to be on my side, dammit! Instead she gave him the cheat codes. It had been a few weeks since Ellis popped up at the hotel thanks to Cadence tipping him off. Prior to that I hadn't seen him in eight days. I'd been prepared to see him at SophieBean's recital and pretend like whatever we had been doing for the past six months had finally come to an end. Then

Cadence just had to open her big mouth and somehow I ended up with my ankles near my ears by the night's end. Then he pulled that broken car shit at the recital and we ended up spending *that* night together as well. A slight shudder traveled through my body as I remembered that night Cadence sent him to me.

Something felt different about the way Ellis touched me. Each graze of his hand on my skin felt like he was trying to tell me something. Our normal frenetic sex was lazy and languid, peppered with long kisses and sweet caresses. I'd chalked it up to our slightly inebriated state, but for him to then double down and drop the bomb that he wasn't sleeping with anyone else in the sober light of day? That shit just left me in a whole whirl of confusion. I mean I was ecstatic that my chance of catching an STD was lessened, but I didn't know what to make of these quasi-monogamous relationship traits Ellis was displaying.

"Is that any way to talk to the mother of your future goddaughter slash babyniece?"

"You don't even know you're having a girl."

"Oh, I know all right. Call it a mother's intuition. I feel it in my shundo, just like I feel you and Ellis should cut the bullshit and get together for real."

"So be sure to let Geoff know he's getting a junior because your mother's intuition is broken. Irreparable, even..."

"Actually, it isn't Ellis that needs to cut the bull. He made his intentions clear. So, what's the holdup, Bee?"

"Made his intentions clear to whom exactly?"

"You, heffa! Let's not play this game," Cadence said, while reaching for the bottle to refill her water glass.

I opened my mouth to respond, but I honestly didn't know what to say. I could lie and say I didn't know his

intentions, but I knew. This man who I'd longed for over
half of my adult life was sitting here gift wrapped for me,
but I couldn't seem to rip that paper to shreds. I was
perfectly fine with things being the way that they initially
started, the occasional booty call to sate a need. But somewhere along the line, those "WYD?" calls and texts turned
into "just wanted to hear your voice" and "I miss you" and
unscheduled drop by visits.

But this was Ellis. The man who I'd witnessed take two
women on a date on the same night, at the same restaurant. The man who said he'd never settle down and get
married. The man who was known on our college campus
as BC...Black Clooney for the sheer number of women to
whom he gave the "you can't lock this down" speech. No
matter what it seemed like he was showing me, history
always reminded me that he wasn't mine for the taking.
He'd get bored eventually and my heart would be broken.
So I played it cool.

"Well?" Cadence prompted.

"I...it just can't be Ellis."

"Why not? Give me three *good* reasons why it can't be?"

"Who's the judge of the level of good?"

"Stop trying to derail Devorah Nicole and answer the
question. I know he's got The Zing."

The Zing was a term Cade and I came up with to
describe that intense chemical spark that happens
between two people who are destined to spend the rest of
their lives together. It was a silly high school creation that
I'd spent most of my adult life chasing. I dated man after
man, hoping that one of them would possess The Zing.
There had been plenty men with whom I had off the
charts sexual energy, but beyond the bedroom were a bore.
Or men, who challenged me intellectually, but were a

snoozefest in bed. In these few months of screwing, Ellis had not only shown me The Zing, but he'd made me rethink a lot of my long held philosophies about life, careers, and dating, honestly. But I couldn't completely go there with him.

"Biiiiiiiitch, he's got the zing, zap and zow!" I sighed.

"So again I ask you…what the prollem is?"

"The problem is *Ellis*."

"Who you've lusted after ever since you learned the proper definition of the word. Still waiting on three good reasons."

"Fine. Three good reasons—one, he's never been serious about anyone in his entire life. I'm tired of playing the dating game and tryna put marriage on my menu. I can't go all in only to find out he's been using me as a plaything. Two—I've fucked his brother. Three—if whatever we're doing implodes, it could possibly destroy our mothers' friendship."

Rolling her eyes, Cadence held up three fingers and replied, "Debunking in reverse order. If you and Everett breaking up didn't mess up Auntie Im and Auntie Randi's relationship, nothing else would. You didn't fuck Everett. Y'all tried; he barely put the tip in before y'all gave up. Unless you're a dirty liar who has kept the secret of who really took her virginity from her bestie since the womb. Also…you said Everett didn't have The Zing, so that attempt at sex doesn't count…"

"That's not how body counts work, sis," I interrupted.

"Don't interrupt your elder when she's speaking."

"Cade, you're a day older."

"And a day wiser, ho. Don't you forget it. And *finally*, you know what Ellis' intentions toward you are. I can tell you this ain't no fly by night shit for him. And you know that. Which is why your ass is running scared," Cadence said, picking up her glass, taking a long sip of water while she stared at me pointedly.

"What is that supposed to mean?"

"Devorah Nicole, dumb doesn't look good on you, sis."

"I hate when you do this though. You obviously know something I don't."

Because she wasn't romantically interested in either of the Taylor brothers, Cadence had always had a different bond with both of them than I did. She and Ellis were especially close and if I was being honest the shit drove me insane. Prior to dating, Everett had been one of my best friends. That changed slightly after he and Cass got together. It was a natural progression and we were still fairly close now, but Ellis and I had never really connected on more than a superficial level. Until now.

"What I know is you're being foolish and need to stop playing."

I toyed with the strawberry garnishing the rim of my mimosa as I contemplated Cadence's words.

"So you're saying I should go all in?"

"I'm saying at the very least you need to have an adult conversation and figure out what the hell y'all are doing. Because the both of you are getting on my damn nerves pumping me for information about the other."

"He asked you about me? What you tell him?"

Cadence shot me a look that, were I not immune after years of enduring her lethal side eye, would have wounded me. She was saved from responding as the waiter came back with our entrees. We ate in silence for a few moments until I felt Cadence's eyes on me.

"What?"

"If...if you're doing this? You got to go all in, Bee. Lean into it."

"You might wanna tell your boy that because he's the one with less to risk here."

"I think you're equally at risk?"

"Shiiiit, I beg to differ. I don't have a trail of broken hearted suitors up and down the eastern seaboard."

"Nope, just a handful of exes who magically found their soul mates after you stopped keeping them hostage."

"Keeping them hos—whose side are you on here?"

"The side of truth," Cadence said, lifting her glass of water to sip once more, "You should try it once. Maybe it will set you free."

"I can't stand your ass."

"You lie. But I love you, too."

————

I nervously shifted from side to side while waiting for Ellis to open the door. I was following Cadence's stupid advice and leaning into it. After we left brunch, I got a four wing platter wrapped to go and stopped by the liquor store to grab a six-pack of Abita Golden Ale. I didn't know what I was doing, but it felt right. I just knew that I wanted to see Ellis so I made my way to his house. Seeing as how I was still standing on the stoop however, I wondered if he'd wanted to see me.

"Hey."

"Hi."

"This is different," Ellis said with a small smirk on his face.

"Are you...busy?" I asked, nervously biting my lip, hoping he'd say no.

He leaned across the doorframe and shook his head.

"Are you going to invite me in?"

"Depends. Is that Cluck for me?" he said with a hint of humor in his voice.

Oh he wasn't going to make this easy. I guess with the way I had been brushing him off he was well within his rights. So, I'd play the game.

"Yep, a 4 wing platter with macaroni and greens. Extra jalapeno on the side. And Abita Golden Ale."

"Who are you and what have you done with Bee?"

"Let me in and maybe you'll find out," I giggled.

"No seriously, who are you?" he asked, moving aside and ushering me in. He grabbed the Cluck bag and headed immediately to the kitchen. "And it's still hot?"

I stopped to hang my coat and bag in his front closet and slipped off my shoes.

"I just left from brunch with Cadence. I wanted to see you, so I figured I wouldn't come empty handed," I said padding into the kitchen and placing the beer in the fridge, "Good surprise?"

"Great surprise," Ellis replied around a mouthful of chicken.

Normally I would have had a smart comment about him replying to me with a mouth full of food, but I was... hell, I don't know what I was doing. I just wanted to be around him without any undue tension or stress. So instead I walked over to the breakfast nook and took a seat on one of the stools at the bar and watched him eat.

Ellis finished chewing the food in his mouth and said, "Sorry. I know that bothers you when people speak with a mouth full of food."

Guess I hadn't steeled my facial expression as much as I'd thought.

I smiled and replied, "You're good. I get it. Cluck will make you forget your manners."

Ellis just stared. I held his gaze at first until his eyes lingered for longer than I was comfortable with.

"What?"

"You're different. I'm just trying to figure it out."

"I'm me. Still."

His eyes narrowed, "Nah. This must be a trap. You tryna get me all chicken and liquored up so my guard is down and you can take advantage of me. Mmmhmmm. I see right through you, girl."

"You are so damn silly. What were you doing before I came? What you getting into today?"

A sly grin spread across his face and I knew I'd walked right into the line that was surely coming from his mouth.

"You. I'm getting into you, if you let me."

I smiled in spite of myself. "That might be able to be arranged."

Ellis put down the wing he was eating and came over to the breakfast nook. He looked seriously confused.

"Ok. For real. What's up?"

I tried feigning innocence.

"What do you mean?"

"Woman, I been chasing your for months, attempting to woo the fuck outta you and you've given me the run around. Today you show up on my doorstep with chicken and my favorite brew. Now you're offering yourself up to me." He lifted a hand to feel my forehead. "Nope, temperature isn't elevated. Did you bump your head in the last twenty four hours?"

"This is mad dramatic, Ellis. Why can't you just lean into it?"

Circling the breakfast nook to sit in the stool next to

me, Ellis nodded. He pulled my stool closer to his, so that his legs encased mine. One of his hands held my right hand, while the other rested on my left thigh, absently drawing circles. That light touch caused a shudder to run through my body.

"Aight. So what does leaning in entail? Because I'm pretty sure I've resembled a young Mike Jackson in Smooth Criminal with all the leaning I've been doing for the past six months while you fronted me off."

I laughed, "Can you be serious?"

"I am being serious. So, the leaning..." Ellis prompted.

Honestly, I had no idea what the hell leaning in even looked like. I just knew that I was tired of denying myself pleasure. Tired of acting like I didn't want this man as badly as I did. So really it was more like giving in instead of leaning in. But God, I couldn't possibly tell him that. Fuck no.

"The leaning in means I've given up my hoes for you."

Ellis threw his head back in laughter. I loved watching him laugh. It was like his entire body was amused. Head thrown back, shoulders shaking as his mouth gaped open and a low rumbling laugh emerged. He got up from the stool and went back to the counter where his food was. I watched as he wrapped it all up, placing the food in the refrigerator. He grabbed two bottles of the beer and the magnetized bottle opener. He gripped both bottles and the opener in one hand as he circled back by the breakfast nook, grabbing my left hand with his free one. He led me into the den, sitting down on the couch and patted his lap for me to sit. I rolled my eyes and chose to sit beside him instead.

"There's my girl."

I warmed at the sound of those words. *His girl*. God, I

wish. Ellis handed me one of the bottles of beer and I took a sip immediately. Prior to beginning this liaison, I could count the number of times I had willingly drank beer. I thought it was disgusting, but Ellis soon taught me that drinking shitty national label brand domestics would have anyone thinking all beer was disgusting. He introduced me to the world of craft brewing and all of the delightful flavors of ales, sours, radlers, and stouts.

Ellis draped an arm around me and turned on the television. We sat there in silence until I finally said, "So if we're gonna really do this I have a couple rules."

Muting the television Ellis drawled, "Now why doesn't that surprise me? Aight hit me."

"Hit you?"

"Yeah, hit me with your best shot. Gimme the catch so I can talk you out of it."

I leaned back a little, sort of shrugging his arm from around my shoulder so I could turn to face him. As I turned, he grabbed my hand to keep me close.

"Why do you keep doing that?"

"Doing what?"

"Putting your hands on me. Not letting me be further than an arm's reach away. Every time we're together. It's kind of annoying."

Ellis dropped my hand immediately. Confusion and hurt were evident in his eyes as he shifted to turn toward me.

"Is that one of your rules?" he asked, dryly.

The playful mood that had filled the room suddenly shifted. Tension eased in and I became instantly regretful of my word choice.

"El," I said, grasping his forearm, "It's not like—"

"Oh, it's okay when you initiate. Got it. Next rule?"

"Maybe we should discuss this later. You seem...upset."

"Because I am upset. So you're not completely oblivious. Good. Next rule."

"Nope. Nah. I'm not...I can't do this with you like this."

Ellis scoffed and reared back.

"Me like...hey, you know what. Maybe you should go."

"Go?"

"Yeah I..." Ellis breathed deeply and ran a hand over his closely cropped hair, "We should probably just...I don't see this going well right now. Can you just...look can we talk about this tomorrow?"

"You're putting me out?"

"Yes," Ellis said, simply, "I'm upset and trying to do the mature thing here."

"The mature thing would be to talk this out. See... maybe I shouldn't be leaning in if you're going to dismiss me every time I say something you don't like."

"It's more than that, Bee and you know it. You say shit to piss me off damn near day. Normally I just take it in stride. Chalk it up to Devorah being Devorah. But today... I just...can you please go? I'll call you tomorrow."

"Or you could not call at all. I don't have time for this hot and cold shit."

"Hot and cold? Oh like you playing me off right now when I'm just tryna be close to you? Hot and cold like telling me you're leaning in and then saying that when I touch you it's annoying. Hot and cold like...Devorah, please."

"I didn't say—" I started, but quickly trailed off. Fuck I did say that. It wasn't what I meant, but damnit, I had to own it.

Ellis stared blankly.

"I didn't mean it. Like that, you know. I...I wasn't saying your touch was annoying."

"You work in marketing, Devorah. You're more than familiar with word meanings and their intent. So...you meant it. And one day we'll get to the bottom of why you meant it. But not today. Because now I'm annoyed and I'd really just like you to go."

Ellis' voice sounded cold and detached; almost robotic. He walked toward the front and retrieved my belongings for me. Shit. He was really putting me out. How we got from an offhand comment I thought sounded like a joke to here had me confused...and a little scared. Here I was finally ready to go all in and once again I sabotaged myself. I knew I had to let him cool off. I grabbed my coat and bag from him, quickly donning both and walking toward the foyer. I stopped to put on my shoes as Ellis watched, standing in the doorjamb that separated the foyer from the living room. I could see the hurt still in his gaze as we made eye contact. I wanted nothing more than to be able to talk this out and get over the hump, but I could tell by his stance, arms folded over his chest; legs braced apart slightly, that he wouldn't be receptive to anything I had to say right now. Hell I didn't even know how I would even begin to apologize. I nodded to him and turned to walk out of the front door.

"Hey."

Ellis' voice stopped me dead in my tracks. I turned back to face him.

"I really am going to call you tomorrow. I just...I need a moment to sort this out, Bee."

I nodded once again and turned to leave. I was hesitant to say anything since my big mouth had caused this tension. When I got into my car, I noticed Ellis still standing in the doorway, making sure I took off safely. I lifted a hand in salute and backed out of his driveway. He nodded once in return. I pressed the voice activated command button on my steering wheel to make a call.

Please say a command after the tone.

Call Cadence Garner.

Which number would you like to dial for Cadence Garner?

Call Cadence Garner mobile.

Calling Cadence Garner mobile.

I was greeted by Cadence answering her phone with a deep sigh.

"Hey."

"What did you do?"

"Um…hi, hello to you, too."

"Nope, no time for pleasantries. Our plan was perfect. You had your script, the bribe, and everything was perfect. You should be face down ass up right about now instead of calling me from your car."

"How did you know I was in—"

"I can hear the background noise. So what did you do? How did you fuck up?"

"Wait a minute. Why does it have to be me that fucked up? Why do you assume Ellis didn't?"

"Because I know your ass lives to sabotage your own happiness. I'm not asking again. And I'm not responding again until you tell me what you did."

"Seriously, Cade? You're giving me the silent treatment via phone?"

Her labored breathing coming through the line was all I heard.

"I don't. I don't know what I did, honestly."

"That's bullshit."

"No it isn't. We were cool. I was just about to start the

lean in speech that we talked about and then he flipped on me and put me out."

"He put you out? Nah...what did you do?"

I was growing increasingly annoyed with Cadence thinking that this had to be my fault. Despite Ellis saying my comment about him touching me being annoying was what set him off, I didn't understand why. I thought we were in a place where I could be perfectly honest with him, but I guess not. At any rate, I didn't have time for this shit from him or from Cadence.

"I didn't do shit."

I briefly ran back the situation, not leaving out a single detail. Cadence remained quiet on the line.

"So you..." Cadence trailed off.

"I swear if you say this is my fault," I started.

"It's not wholly your fault, but—"

"I'm gonna pull an Ellis and end this here. I can't do this right now. I'll call you later."

I pressed the end call button and turned up the radio. The playlist I was listening to on my way to Ellis' automatically piped into the car. Ugh, the last song I wanted to hear right now was Beyoncé's "Love on Top". I pressed the voice-activated button to change the playlist.

"Play I Can't Stand Your Ass playlist."

Playing I Can't Stand Your Ass.

The first song on the playlist was Chanté Moore's "Bitter". I drove and sang my heart out all the way home.

ELLIS

"You put her out?" Cadence's laughter rang through my car loudly.

She called while I was on my way back to the office from a client lunch. I was pretty sure Bee wasted no time calling her yesterday and was surprised Cadence held off on calling me this long. I was sure that I would get read the riot act by her immediately for putting Devorah out yesterday, justified or not. I was mostly over it, but still giving myself some time before I talked about it with Bee. I didn't want our phone conversation to become an extension of what could have been a huge blow up yesterday.

"Your girl is out of her mind, CadyMac. I might not be cut out for this shit."

Cadence's laughter went up in pitch, now resembling a scream. I waited for her to get her composure. After a few moments, her giggles subsided into silence.

"You done?"

She released a breath, "Yeah, I think I am. You really told her to get out of your house though? El, I told you... kid gloves!"

"Nope, I'm not with the kid gloves bullshit any longer. Be clear, I care about her a lot. Probably more than I should be admitting to you before admitting to her, but I won't be made to seem like a stalker or something. I don't have to convince women to be with me. I don't have to work this hard for a piece of..."

"Hold up, playa. You told me this was some real shit. That's the *onnnnnly* reason I agreed to help you out. If you're playing me Ellis Stacey Taylor, I swear to God I'll cut your ass off right now."

"Chill out. I just told you I care about her..."

"Nah, nah. I don't want to hear that *I care about her* shit, El. Because if you cared about the girl, you would stop being so cloak and dagger with her. Stringing her along for all this time."

"What are you talking about, Cade? I've been nothing but upfront for these last few months."

"This shit goes back further than that and you know it, El. Cut the shit. This goes back to that summer Uncle James & Auntie Im divorced."

"What the hell are you talking about, CadyMac? Nothing happened with us that summer. I mean, Bee and I talked...a lot, but it never went beyond talking."

"You're being super obtuse right now, my G. Cut it out. You know that damn girl was halfway in love with you already. That summer sealed the damn deal."

"Cadence, that was over ten years ago, though. She's moved on for sure. For damn sure because I can barely get her to give me play now."

"I said what I said. You know her, Ellis. You know this is a front."

"Do I know her though? As far as I can tell it's a damn

good front. She got me thinking that she just wants my dick on demand and that's it."

"Because as far as she knows that's all you're offering, Sir Hoes A Lot."

"Tales of my manwhoring have been greatly exaggerated," I deadpanned.

"Yeah, yeah whatever. So you know you just made this shit worse right? She's Fat Joe and Remy Ma right now."

"What the hell does that even mean?"

"She's leaning back."

"I hate this reference. Hate even more that I asked you to explain it. But how bad is it?"

"So bad that she put me out of her car phone once I tried to tell her both of y'all were at fault."

"Wait a minute how were we—"

"You don't think putting her out and telling her you'd call her tomorrow was overreacting, El?"

I quietly pondered the question. Devorah insulted me and my subsequent reaction wasn't over the top *to me*. However, I knew that if we had continued talking, I would have gotten even more upset and possibly caused irreparable damage. That was the last thing I wanted to do. I needed to create some space so I could calmly tell her why her comment set me off. In hindsight, it probably wasn't the most mature move.

"Aight. I'll accept my part in this. I probably shouldn't have put her out. But you do get *why* I put her out right?"

"I definitely do. Which is what I was trying to explain to her before she hung up on me. Both of y'all are getting on my nerves to be quite honest."

"I hate to keep putting you in the middle of this."

"Then stop."

We were silent for a bit then both burst out laughing.

Cadence knew that was impossible given how often she talked to the both of us. She and Bee had been best friends since they were swimming in amniotic fluid, so it was inevitable that she'd talk to her about her man troubles... or lack thereof. I would admit an uptick in the frequency of our chats since Devorah and I had gotten together, but it was her damn fault for being so accommodating. If Cadence didn't want to be caught in the middle she could have easily told both of us to shut up. She never would though because according to her we were canon OTP. Whatever the hell that meant.

"You know a phone call isn't gonna cut it, right?"

"Which is why I had purple and white calla lilies delivered this morning with a note, *handwritten might I add,* letting her know to expect a call from me this afternoon."

"Oh, you're good," Cadence replied, a bit of awe in her voice.

"I told you I ain't new to this, I'm true to this."

"Well, why you wasting time on the line with me? Don't you have a call to make?"

I glanced at the dash and saw that it was a quarter of two. The note I sent with the flowers this morning told her to expect my call by three. I'd wanted to give myself more than enough time to make it through my client lunch and get settled back in at the office.

"We're not scheduled 'til three, but I just pulled back into the lot at the plantation. Got a couple things I need to take care of before I make that call, so I'll talk to you later."

"May the odds ever be in your favor, brother."

———

I'd never been nervous to call a woman. Not even back in the sixth grade when I got Heather Daniels to give me her number despite being an eighth grader whose sights were set on high school dudes. I'd just ushered the lead graphic designer out of my office and had five minutes before I was supposed to call Bee. I didn't have a clue of what I was going to say and it had me thrown to be honest. I'd always had a slick mouth that was skilled at convincing the ladies to give me what I wanted. This was different, though. Heaving a sigh, I picked up the phone, dialing Devorah's office number.

"This is Devorah."

"Hey Bee."

I heard a slight intake of air on the other end of the phone before she answered.

"Hi."

"Did I catch you at a bad time?"

"Nope. I blocked off three o'clock 'til three oh seven as give Ellis time to grovel time on my calendar."

"Seven minutes? Damn, that's a whole lot of please baby please, Bee."

She laughed softly. I took this as a sign that we were good.

"Thank you for the flowers, by the way. They're beautiful."

"Not as beautiful...nah, I can't even finish that corny shit."

Bee laughed loudly and said, "Thank you. Because had you done that, I'm certain I would have never let you inside me again."

"And what a pity that would have been. Hey...you busy tonight? I don't want to do this over the phone. I'd rather be looking you in the eyes as I apologize.

Besides...we never got through the rest of the leaning in rules."

"About that..." Devorah started.

"Nope, save it for later. Is seven cool? I'll drop by after the gym."

"Showered, hopefully."

"Really, Bee? So seven...?"

"Seven is fine. I'll have dinner waiting."

"Aight. I'll see you then."

Bee paused briefly then said, "See you later, El."

We hung up and I went back to the pile of RFPs on my desk that I needed to complete and submit before the end of the week. I'd been tasked with recruiting a few more local businesses to work with our firm for their marketing needs. We were trying to break into the small business sector, primarily targeting minority owned businesses. A larger firm whose focus was broadening the level of service that we provided to local start-ups had recently acquired my company. My team was researching businesses and crafting requests for proposals to pitch to their leadership teams. This kind of put me in direct competition with Devorah's firm, as cross-pollination was inevitable when you have two similarly structured companies trying to acquire the same customers. Luckily, since Bee was a creative, we never went directly head to head. The rest of the workday passed fairly quickly as I delegated assignments to the sub-teams I supervised.

———

I pulled up to Devorah's house slightly before seven. I could barely focus on my workout trying to parse together what the hell I was going to say in this apology. I still didn't think I was completely in the wrong, but I was taking Cadence's advice about handling Bee with kid gloves seriously. One thing was for sure though; I was leaving here with a better understanding of what the hell was going on in her head. I grabbed the bottle of wine I'd bought from the grocery store and walked up the short walkway to the front door. Just as I raised a hand to press the doorbell, the door opened and a mass of red hair came barreling toward me.

"UNCLE ELLLLLLLLL!"

I gathered my niece in my arms for a hug and asked, "Hey Sweetpea, what are you doing here?"

Before she could answer, Cassidy, whom I hadn't noticed was right behind her said, "We were just leaving. Thanks again, Dev. Heyyyyy, El." She turned back toward Bee who was standing in the entry way between the kitchen and hallway that lead to the front door. They exchanged a series of blinks and eyebrow raises before Cass and Sophie shuffled out of the door.

"What was that about?"

"Oh. Cass got caught up at work and asked me to pick up Soph so she wouldn't be charged extra for being late."

"Nah, nah...I'm talking about—"

"What kinda wine is that?" Bee said and advanced toward me to take the bag.

I handed it over and shrugged my coat off to hang on the coat rack. Bee had already walked back toward the kitchen, so I joined her there. I smelled spaghetti; so going with the red wine was the right choice. I had a fifty-fifty chance though. Bee could only cook two meals well; both of them were pasta based – with either a red or white sauce. I made myself useful and set the table. After I placed the last of the silverware down, I looked up to see

Bee staring at me with a look on her face I couldn't quite place.

"I can't figure you out," she said finally, "Can you grab the salad out the fridge? I'll bring this over so we can chow down."

I grabbed the salad and dressing from the refrigerator and brought it over to the table. We plated our meals and tucked into eating. Conversation was sparse as we stuffed our faces, but we talked around the reason I had come over here anyway. Instead we chose to stay on neutral topics like work, Sophie, and the gym. After finishing our food, we cleared the table. Devorah loaded the dishwasher while I sat in the living room area waiting for her, at her insistence. As I sat waiting, I thought about what the hell I was going to say to get back in her good graces and get us over this stupid little fight.

"You look like you're deep in thought," Devorah said, as she sat down next to me.

I hadn't even heard her approach.

"Either you're a ninja or this carpet's padding muffles every damn thing. I didn't even hear you come in here."

Devorah threw her head back with laughter. She quickly sobered and turned toward me.

"Before you start, can I say something?"

I was taken aback, but intrigued, "Shoot."

She inched a little closer, fidgeting with her nails. I maintained eye contact until her gaze fell onto her hands. She released a small breath and then raised her head to look me in the eyes once again.

"So I just want to say that I was kind of a jerk the other night and I'm sorry that I made you put me out."

The shock at her apology must have shown on my face because she just continued talking.

"I just…I sometimes don't know what to say and that was a prime foot in mouth moment. I didn't realize the impact my words would make. You always seem so nonchalant and I didn't realize how harshly they may have been received."

She grabbed my hand and continued, "I'm only annoyed because when your hands are on me I can hardly think straight and to be frank, I don't like that feeling. I don't like being out of control."

I tucked that tidbit of information away to revisit later.

"So. Yeah. Sorry for being a jackass," she finished, breaking eye contact once again.

I grabbed her chin, bringing her eyes up to meet mine before I spoke.

"We both overreacted. I'll own up to my part in that. So if you accept my apology for kicking you out like you were Pamela James, then we can start this relationship on a clean slate."

A small smile crept onto her face, while her eyes held a bit of confusion.

"Relationship?"

"Yep. Relationship. Let's cut the bullshit, Bee. Despite whatever cloudy ass words you want to classify it — *leaning in or whatever* — this is a relationship. We've been exclusively screwing each other's brains out for at least six months, *albeit inconsistently*…your fault…"

"Wait," she interrupted, "Exclusively?"

"Have you been with someone else?"

"Well no."

"And neither have I, so that's how exclusivity works."

"And how is the inconsistency my fault?"

"Really?" I replied, rolling my eyes.

"Fine. FINE. You're right. But…"

"No buts, we're doing this. Full steam ahead. I'm talking fancy restaurants, sexy lingerie, all that shit."

"But you know we still can't tell our families, right? I don't want—"

"If you think Cassidy didn't call Everett to tell him as soon as she breeched your doorstep, I've got a beach house to sell you in Idaho," I laughed.

"If she hasn't spilled the beans by now, I think I'm good."

"Wait...she knew?"

"She's my best friend, El!"

"Cadence is your best friend. And, I thought, the only person in our immediate circle beyond us who knew."

"You can't tell me that Cade's the only person you've talked about this."

"Besides the point. The person I told is not married into the family!"

"Ah ha! I knew it! Oh my god, who else knows?"

"Trey, but *he's my best friend, Bee*!" I said, mimicking her tone for justifying telling Cassidy.

"Har de har. But for real, can we hold off on telling the family until we see where this is going? I just..." Devorah broke off and looked away again.

I grabbed her arm, pulling her closer.

"You just..." I prompted.

"I just need a little time is all. Can you give me a little time?"

"I dunno, Bee. I mean...I might need some incentive to keep my mouth shut."

A sneaky little smile crossed her lips before she slowly licked them. She stood, moving directly in front of me. Using the tip of her foot, she nudged my legs apart and stood between them. Not breaking eye contact, she grabbed the hem of her dress, slowly raising it. As the hem traveled up her thigh, so did my gaze. She soon revealed a set of black, lacy panties and a matching bra, which barely restrained what, was undeniably my favorite part of Bee's body, her beautiful breasts.

As she whipped the dress over her head, my hands charted a course beginning at her thighs, over her ass and up to cup those mounds. Devorah's eyes slid closed as I teased her nipples into hardened peaks.

"Mmmmm," she moaned as I moved forward, tugging her bra up slightly to take a peak into my mouth, while still stimulating the other with my left hand. My right hand traveled south, skimming down her stomach to the waistband of her panties.

She brushed my hand away, stepping back slightly. She was a sight, chest heaving, bra twisted, eyes sparkling with barely restrained lust. She adjusted her bra and turned to walk out of the room. I sat there on the couch until I heard her ask, "You comin'?"

5

DEVORAH

"So what were the other rules?" Ellis' low rumble pulled me out of the orgasm induced haze I'd been in. I was dozing off when he asked the question to which I had no definite answer. The only real rule I had regarding the rollout of this relationship was how it would eventually be revealed to the family. The last thing I needed was Imogene Landon-Lee calling me and going on about how good girls don't hop from brother to brother. Or how I should have never gave Everett to that damn ginger girl for the millionth time.

"Well...er...um..." I stalled.

"Wait a damn minute. There aren't any rules beyond *don't tell my mama* are there? Auntie Im got you that shook?" Ellis laughed.

"It's not just my mama I'm worried about..."

"Well who else? Certainly not Everett."

"Hell no. That fool probably already knows because Cass can't hold water."

"I thought you said..."

"I said nothing; you assumed," I laughed.

"So who else? Certainly not *my* mama."

I remained quiet, playing with the scalloped lace edges of my sheets. That was exactly who had me shook. Don't get me wrong, I definitely didn't want the judgment from my mother, but I could just ignore her ass for a few days and she'd get past it. But Auntie Randi...I couldn't be the lil heffa who messed around with both of her sons. I'd always been closer to her than Cadence's mom Auntie Berta because of our shared love of dance. Auntie Randi was the one who encouraged my mom to put me into Hurston Dance Company after she saw me messing around with choreography on my own around the house. When Everett and I broke up, Auntie Randi had nothing bad to say, but I always felt like she was a bit disappointed that I wouldn't become her daughter-in-law, popping out little dancing grandbabies. Don't get me wrong, she loved Cassidy, but they were about as opposite as two folks could get. Thank goodness Sophie Bean inherited her grandma's dance genes.

"For real, Bee? Quit playin', you know Miranda loves her some Devorah."

"Yeah, but will she love the Devorah that's fucked both of her sons?"

"Bee, just the tip doesn't count."

"It totally doe---wait! You know about that? *Oh my goooooooood*," I moaned, burying my face in my hands and turning away from Ellis.

Everett and I swore we wouldn't tell anyone about our failed sexcapades. I mean I'd told Cade, obviously, but he had to know that was a given. There was rarely anything that I didn't tell her. But that didn't mean he could tell his brother. Ellis grabbed my shoulder and pulled me into an embrace, kissing my forehead as he chuckled.

"Baby, that was over ten years ago. Besides...I won anyway! You let me get all up in them..."

"Stop. Ew. Do not finish that sentence or you will never get all up in me ever again."

"Yeah right," Ellis drawled, running his hand down my body to cup my ass.

"Stop tryna distract me. I'm serious though. Please let's just chill on letting the old heads know about whatever this thing is."

"This *thing* being our relationship. Say it with me, Bee. Our rela...actually, scratch that. I'm about to make you take an oath. Repeat after me. I, Devorah Nicole Lee..."

I rolled my eyes, pushing against Ellis slightly to loosen his embrace. He pulled me in even closer, locking a leg around mine to keep me in place. I looked up to see him waiting with one eyebrow cocked.

"All right, fine. I, Devorah Nicole Lee..."

"Do solemnly swear..."

"Do solemnly swear..."

"That I am in a relationship with Ellis Stacey Taylor..."

"That I am in..." I paused.

Ellis just looked at me, with his brow still raised.

I smirked, "All right, all right, I'll quit fucking with you. That I am in a relationship with Ellis Stacey Taylor..."

My heart damn near burst outta my chest after saying that line. Lord, it was something I never thought in life I'd be saying, let alone repeating in some crazy ass oath Ellis had me taking. Pretty sure that I was grinning like a loon at this point as well.

"Who is knocking the bottom out that thang."

"I'm not repeating that."

Outloud that is, because he was certainly knocking the top, bottom, middle and sides out of that thang. *Whew.*

"You know it's true. I know it's true. It's fine. You don't have to say it."

"I can't stand you."

"Lies you tell, woman!"

———

Ellis left my house late that night, so waking up the next morning to get to work was a struggle. Part of me wanted to tell him to just stay and call off with me, but I knew that wasn't logical because I was working on the creative properties for this project my girl Celena was managing. We were set to finalize the campaign by the close of business today, so I specifically scheduled the bulk of my day to ensure all of the deliverables were to the specifications that the persnickety ass marketing manager at Parker & Associates had laid out for us. Celena was one of the first people who quickly welcomed me with open arms when I started at Jamieson & Weil, so I always made sure to deliver her goods without delay. Thankfully, I'd finished most of the difficult illustration work on the logo she needed for the client's landing page; so today was going to be consumed with creating the look in about five different color ways because Robert Parker was unable to "fully see the vision" unless he saw it displayed in all five color combinations that he had been envisioning. A love for what I do and a hefty paycheck kept me from getting exasperated with these folks daily as they expected me to cater to their ridiculous whims.

I reached over to the nightstand to shoot off a text letting my manager Teresa know I'd be pulling in a little late this morning and noticed a text from Ellis. I fired off the text to Teresa and then proceeded to read Ellis' text.

Opening up the thread, I noticed it was actually a short video. Pressing play, I immediately broke into a grin. Ellis' handsome face filled the screen while he talked about how he wished that he could have stayed the night and how next time he'll be better prepared. Then the camera started to slowly pan as he kept talking about how he woke up this morning thinking about me and *oh my god*. Yep. Definitely his hand on his dick showing me how much he was thinking about me. The camera panned back up and Ellis was still talking, but I'd be goddamned if I knew what he actually said at the end. My mind was still stayed on that dick. Shaking it off, I sent Ellis a text.

You know you ain't shit for that video right?

Did you get to the end? —Ellis Taylor

Yes I got to the end, fool.

So why am I getting words from you instead of a video in return? — Ellis Taylor

I pulled up the video again, fast-forwarding to the end to listen to what he was saying this time instead of concentrating on...*other things*. I chuckled as Ellis detailed exactly how I could show him I missed him, too, if I had the time.

I'm not sending you that.

Took you a minute. You thought about it, didn't you? Probably watched the whole damn video again and over there playin witcha self right now. Nasty ass. — Ellis Taylor

Shut upppppp. No, I'm not. I'm actually on my way to the shower.

Word? Gimme fifteen and I can be there to share it. — Ellis Taylor

I bit down on my lip, the offer sounded tempting but I knew that if he came back I would certainly not make it into the office today.

Coulda saved that time if you'd stayed.

A brotha didn't wanna wear out his welcome. — Ellis Taylor

Could literally never happen.

Noted. — Ellis Taylor

I breezed into work slightly earlier than I'd told Teresa and literally ran into Celena as I was entering the building.

"Whoa Cel, where's the fire?"

"Parker & Associates. Just heard Urban Current might be tryna undercut us. So I'm on an ambush mission. Not on my watch!" Celena called over her shoulder, hot-footing it to the parking garage.

Celena had been dating the son of the owner of P&A, Jake, so I was sure someone was about to get an unexpected and unpleasant visit from his not so happy girlfriend. P&A had been clients of ours for years, and certainly couldn't be swayed by whatever tricks Urban Current decided to pull out the bag. I knew Urban Current's focus has shifted a bit with their recent acqui- sition. I hope this didn't end up in any hunger games ass bullshit between firms. We were perfectly fine when their focus was national while ours was more local and grassroots. The last thing we needed was them encroaching on our territory. And the last thing I needed was unnecessary strife between Ellis and me. I sat my things down in my office and then headed over to Tere- sa's office.

"Hey, what's up with the P&A joint? I just literally ran into Celena on her way to ambush Jake. I thought we were good? I was gonna begin the final colorization of their logos today."

Teresa ran her fingers through her already tousled curls. "Girl, we came in this morning and it was like a damn fire drill. I don't know how, but somebody at Urban Current got Robert Sr.'s ear and will be submitting RFPs for the campaign we were supposedly locked in for."

"Well isn't that something."

"Some bull is what it is. But that's our bad. We took Jake at his word instead of having signed contracts in hand."

"Wait. The renewals hadn't been signed despite me working my ass off to create logo after logo? Please tell me that is not what you're saying, Teresa."

I'd spent weeks drawing and redrawing logos to the specifications of a very particular marketing manager for Parker and Associates, who also happened to be the other son of the owner, Robert Jr. It was my understanding that we'd had already signed renewal contracts. I was handling the Parkers with a baby soft touch because I knew they were one of our biggest contracts that brought us a great deal of revenue. If all of the work I'd done for the past six weeks was for nothing, I swear to God…

"So what's the game plan? Beyond Cel bopping her man over the head until he rescinds his RFP requests from Urban Current?"

Teresa laughed, "Thomas wants the team to meet at eleven to come up with a plan of attack."

"Now y'all know I do pictures; not words. Do I even have to come to this?"

"Yep," Teresa said, "You need to know whether or not you should keep drawing on your little etch-a-sketch."

"Hey!"

Teresa laughed even harder. I heaved a sigh and left Teresa's office. A part of me didn't want to even begin work on these color ways in the off chance that all of my work would be for nothing, but I also didn't want to be caught with my pants around my ankles if this was just a scare tactic to ensure we were willing to fight to keep Parker as a client. I settled in, opened up Illustrator, and began working.

———

"Hey girl...you busy?" Celena popped her head into my office at a little before eleven.

"Nope, just getting ready to shut down and head to the conference room. What's up?"

I went back to saving the logo drafts and closing down the program.

"Your boy works at Urban Current, right? Elliott?"

"Ellis. Yeah, why?"

"I need you to find out why P&A is all of a sudden waffling on what was sure to be a done deal."

My hands hovered over my keyboard, about to lock it as I said, "You need me to do who and what now? Why can't you ask Jake?"

"JP is...we're..." Celena sighed, moving into my office and taking a seat in one of the chairs in front of my desk.

"Cel...you can't come in here minutes before we're supposed to be brainstorming asking me to be inch high private eye."

"Look, we'll talk about it after the meeting, but just know...JP isn't a resource anymore."

I stared at her, eyebrows raised.

"Ooooookay."

"Yeah girl, this isn't a conversation to be had here. Or without drinks. Actually, what do you have brewing this evening? Wanna go down to Imbibe and have a glass or three of wine?"

"Absolutely. I was just going to go home and do that same thing. Might as well do it with a friend...and hot gossip."

Lowering her eyes, Celena heaved another sigh. Normally, Cel was an upbeat, perky lil somebody or other, but really looking at her now she seemed...defeated.

"Maybe we shouldn't be having this convo at Imbibe. Why don't you just come by the house after work, so we can really get into it."

"You sure?"

"Sis. You look like somebody just stole your bike. I am absolutely sure that we need to have this conversation anywhere, but in public. Come on; let's get into this doggone meeting before Tom sends someone for us. You know he trips if you're thirty seconds late."

I grabbed a notebook, rounded my desk, and headed toward the door.

When we got into the conference room, Tom sat there with a dour look on his face. I looked at the clock, we had thirty seconds to spare, so I wasn't so sure why Tom looked so annoyed. As soon as everyone else filed into the room, however, I learned the reason for Tom's disposition.

"As of 10:07 today, Parker and Associates is no longer a client of this firm. For reasons that they refused to disclose, they wanted to terminate their relationship with us effective immediately."

People began to murmur about the abruptness of this news and Tom's unusually calm demeanor. I was pissed, but tried not to let it show on my face. I'd spent weeks working with that jackass Robert Parker, Jake's older brother and heir to the Parker throne for nothing. I glanced over at Celena and she looked shell-shocked. So she clearly had no idea this was coming. *Oh boy...*

———

"I'm sorry. Run that by me one more time."

We were sitting in my den, TV on in the background ignored as we sipped our way through the second bottle of Petite Syrah.

"You heard me. I pull up to P&A thinking this was all a misunderstanding and I'd be able to get everything ironed out with JP. I'm barely through the revolving doors before I'm being escorted right back out."

"Like, 'ma'am can you please leave the premises escorted out'?"

"More like 'I hate to have to do this to you, Cel', but definitely a 'we're going to have to ask you to leave' type deal."

"I thought you were cool with that security guard dude, Petey, or whoever."

I'd accompanied the sales and marketing teams to Parker and Associates a few times. Every time I remembered Celena and that Petey guy having extensive conversations about everything under the sun as we waited for the Parker trio to be ready to meet. To know that he was the one who put her out seemed suspect as hell.

"I am. Which is why it wasn't more of a scene. Pete tried to be as discreet as possible. Told me that I was flagged in the system as high risk. Whatever the hell that means."

"And Jake isn't answering your calls?"

"Not a single one. I've called him at least twenty-seven times. Even went by his house before I came by here and..." Celena broke off, looking away, tears welling.

"I can't believe the nerve of this motherfucker. You were with him for three years and he just up and pulled this mess? No explanation and has the audacity to fuck with your livelihood? Cel, you know I'm a lover not a fighter, but if you want me to let that nigga know these hands are rated E for everybody, just say the word, sis."

Celena remained silent, still staring off into space with a slight grin on her face.

"I don't even understand though, Dev. We were good. Hadn't seen each other in a few days, but that wasn't unusual. We still talked every day. He just told me last night how much he loved me and now today I'm a fucking risk?"

Slowly, a tear trickled down her cheek. She didn't bother brushing it away, just let it roll until others joined it. She began sobbing softly and I immediately pulled her into a hug. As her body rocked with sobs, I felt so powerless. My friend definitely did not deserve this kind of treatment. Somebody needed to put a foot up in Jake's ass, honestly.

"I'm so serious, Cel. Where's his place? I'll roll up; hit him with The Stevie. Here's your fade, baby. Signed, sealed, delivered—it's yours! Or The Oprah if he got a new ho in there. You get a fade, you get a fade, everybody gets a fade."

Celena pulled back from my embrace, laughing hysterically.

"Why are you so foolish?"

"There we go. I accomplished my mission. I got you to laugh. Fuck him, Cel. I know you're hurting. I know you want answers, but you deserve better than this mess he's pulling."

"I just wish I knew what was even going on in his head."

We finished the bottle of wine, while I caught Celena up on the happenings between Ellis and I over the past few days. I was hesitant to even bring it up, but Cel asked and refused to let it go until I caught her up. She knew about the fight at his house, so I brought her up to speed about the apology and subsequent relationship declaration and oath. She teased me mercilessly about denying my destiny, citing that trite ass "if you love someone let them go; if they come back they're yours" saying. I brushed her off, but was really amazed. Her love life had just been blown to smithereens and instead of languishing in the misery; she was over here encouraging me to go all in with Ellis. I'd never been the hopeless romantic type chick, but that was Celena to the core. I hoped she got the answers she sought from this shitbacle with Jake and eventually would be able to find someone who deserved all the love she had to give.

ELLIS

"Don't you think it's about time you settled down, Scoot?" my mother asked as we sat around the table, eating. I nearly dropped the platter containing the oven-fried chicken that I was passing to Everett. I steadied my grip and passed the plate to my left to a smirking Everett. That smirk let me know that his wife obviously clued him into whatever intel she had on me and Bee.

"Aw, ma, don't start."

"Aw ma, hell. I'm sick of it. Those two," she said, gesturing to Everett, "refuse to gimme anymore grandchildren. I love my SophieBug, but it would be nice to have more than one set of photos to pass around when I get together with the girls."

"Mama, you the only one with photos *to* pass around at this point. Auntie Berta only got sonograms," Everett chimed in.

"And Imogene has none," my father piped up.

"And none of that has anything to do with why this boy thinks he's the black George Clooney. You gonna wait until you're fifty to get married too, Scooter?"

I just shook my head and let her keep talking. It did no good for me to even try to reason with her when she got on a roll. Not only had she regressed to calling me my childhood nickname, but she also had a bug up her butt about some damn grandkids. She'd spend the next twenty minutes outlining all of the reasons that I needed to get my life together, find a girl to marry and pop out some kids in the next six to eight months. This became the topic of conversation about every three weeks at our weekly family dinners. It was so cyclical it was a wonder that she didn't get tired of hassling me about my dating life.

"Ma. I'm only thirty-four, calm down."

"Boy do you know where we were at thirty-four? We'd been married for twelve years and both of you knuckle-heads were in elementary school by then. To my estimation, you and your brother are slow."

"Hey! At least Cass and I have a kid already," Everett laughed.

"Speaking of, where is Cass? She never misses a chance to eat some of mama's cooking."

"She's with Devorah today. But nice try to change the subject though..."

"Thanks, bro," I said, rolling my eyes.

I knew exactly where Cassidy was. Bee was hosting some sort of ladies brunch thing with her friends today. I was hoping Everett would see the comment for the oop it was and slam down that subject change. As usual, my little brother enjoyed seeing my ass get filleted by our mother.

"I'm just saying, I'd like to be mobile when you decide to bless me with my first grandchild is all."

"Yeah, yeah..."

"Get off the boy's back, Ran. Would you rather him have baby mama drama?" Pops said.

Mama huffed, but quieted down. We continued the rest of the meal with Sophie taking over the show, regaling us with stories about the kids at school, her teacher, and dance class. After dinner, Mama ran off with Sophie to practice some moves for yet another performance that was coming up soon. My pops, Everett and I retired to Pops' man cave to watch the game. I'd been jetting right after every family dinner since Bee and I had officially hooked up. This week since Bee had her girls over, I had no reason to book it home immediately. There was nothing waiting on me at home but piles of work anyway.

"So what's her name, son?" my father asked, seemingly out of nowhere.

"Whose name, pops?"

"The one that's got you running outta here barely after you finish the last bite of ya meal every week? Don't give me that bullshit excuse you're giving your mother, either."

Everett laughed, looking at me.

"Pops, I really did get put in charge of a new project at work," I said, not answering the question.

"I don't doubt you did, Ellis. But I know my son. You're too anxious when you're tryna get up outta here. You don't have that crazy ass expression that you normally do when the job got you hemmed up. So it's gotta be a lil filly."

I remained silent, neither confirming nor denying. Everett continued laughing.

"What's so funny, Ev? You met her yet? Why isn't he bringing her 'round here to meet ya mama and me yet? She got a cockeye? One leg shorter than the other? Hump in the back?"

"N-n-nah pops. I don't know n-nothing about any girl. I think it really is some w-work shit," Everett said, unconvincingly.

"And you're obviously lying, Porky."

I laughed loudly at that. Pops hadn't called him that in at least twenty years. Everett was less than amused, however. Growing up, Ev was a lil portly through his preteen years. Combine that with his penchant for stuttering when he wasn't telling the truth and the nickname was born. That goddamn stammer had given me away though. We sat in silence until Pops broke the stalemate.

"Fine. I'll leave it for now. But I'm warning you; your flimsy work excuse won't last much longer. You know how Miranda is. She's about to start parading eligible bachelorettes in front of you at these dinners. So whatever you got going on with your love life, you better get it together fast."

"You gotta hold her off, Pops."

"Now you know good and damn well I can't stop that woman when she's on a roll."

"Dad. For real. I need you to run interference for me. I'm not confirming or denying anything, but I will say that I don't need Miranda Taylor finding me a woman. Not right now. Not in the future."

My dad paused a beat, looking at me curiously for a few minutes.

"Okay."

"Okay? That's it?"

"Yep," he replied, taking a sip of his beer and turning his attention back to the game.

After the game went off, Pops went for his post-dinner nap and Everett and I remained in the man cave.

"So you obviously know," I said.

"Mmmmmmmhmmmmm. You know my wife can't hold water. Told me she saw you at Bee's last week."

"I had no idea Cass even knew, bruh."

"Y'all dating or just fuckin'? Cass ain't know that for sure."

"Everett, chill."

"Man, since when are you a debutante? Don't act like we haven't had worse conversations. Well?"

"I'm not answering that."

Everett just nodded and made an indistinct noise.

"What?"

"Nothin'. Nothing at all, my brother. So what's with the secret squirrel shit?"

"What! There's something your wife didn't tell you? Because I'm sure she knows better than me at this point. Bee doesn't want the fam to know. She thinks Mama and Auntie Im would lose their shit. I told her she was trippin'."

Everett said nothing, looking away to pick up his beer and take a long draw.

"What?"

"She has a point."

"The fuck she does? Why because y'all dated on some kiddie shit back in the day?"

"That *and* the fact that you aren't exactly known for being Mr. Forever. So when you eventually end whatever this is that y'all are doing, it's going to be mad awkward for the entire family, man. Who wants to deal with that shit?"

"And what if I told you that this won't be over any time soon?"

"Then I'd say you might wanna let Bee know because she doesn't have a clue."

"Noted."

———

"Robert Parker is on the line for you, Ellis. Do you want me to transfer him through?" Pauline said.

"Senior or Junior?"

"Junior."

Here we go again. Robert Parker, Jr. was a pain in my ass. I don't know what it was that caused them to leave Jamieson & Weil, but I'll be damned if I didn't wish that they would take their business back. Sighing, I told Pauline to patch him through.

"Ellis, Robert Parker here. Just wanted to touch base and see where you guys were with that logo update I asked for."

"Our graphics team is currently working to implement the changes, Rob. Like I said in the email, I'll get it back to you as soon as possible. I know they have a few things that are high priority and some of the team is out on vacation, so it may be a few days before we're able to get those changes implemented. The timetable isn't changing, right? We're still aiming for the new site to be launched in six weeks, right?"

"Yeah, yeah. Six weeks. I just don't want you all to fall too far behind. Jamieson & Weil never had these issues. I had that fine ass graphic designer over there at my beck and call. Tell her to jump and she asked how high. Damn. Sure hate that Father and Jake decided we needed to work with Urban Current going forward."

I steeled my tongue, seeing as how that "fine ass graphic designer" was my girlfriend and hearing this nigga go on and on about her like this made me wanna punch his entire face in. I hated that I was even put on this damn project, honestly. Carl insisted that it go to me since I was heading up our local business efforts. Roger, my counter-part, could have taken this shit though. I'd rather have dealt with national brands over interactions with this prick.

"Like I said, Rob, we'll get you sorted out in the next few days. Was there anything else you needed? I'm headed to a meeting shortly."

"Robert."

Was this nigga talking to himself?

"Pardon?"

"My name is Robert. You called me Rob."

You gotta be shitting me.

"Right. Anything else you need?"

"That'll be all for now. If I need anything else, I'll call back," Robert said, hanging up.

Rude ass bastard. I pressed the intercom to alert Pauline.

"Yes?"

"If that idiot calls back again today, don't put him through."

I could hear the suppressed laughter in Pauline's voice as she agreed to my demand. I checked with the lead graphic designer via email to get a more precise idea of when they'd have deliverables ready for this chump so I could avoid further interaction. As soon as I heard back from them, I'd email Rob...*oh excuse me*, Robert back so he'd stop calling me.

————

"How did you deal with that motherfucker, babe?"

We were in the middle of eating lunch when I asked Bee that question. I'd gotten a few curious looks when I showed up looking for Devorah. I wasn't sure if that was because I worked for *The Competition* or because no other man had come into the Jamieson & Weil offices for her prior to me. The petty side of me wanted it to be the latter. Bee seemed pleasantly surprised by my pop up. I'd come over to take her out to lunch, but was summarily turned down. Instead we'd ordered in some Cluck and commandeered a conference room to chow down.

"Which motherfucker is that, El?"

"Rob Parker, Jr. That guy is a head case."

"Oh that guy," she replied, rolling her eyes, "Not having to deal with him anymore is the only upside to us no longer having the Parker account. He used to call me at least six times a day with design suggestions."

"Oh, so I should feel special because he's only calling me three times daily?"

"Low key, I think he had a thing for me and assumed since my girl was dating his brother that he had a shot, but..." she trailed off, shuddering.

"Yeah, he definitely had a thing for you. He manages to bring you up in nearly every damn conversation. He's lucky I haven't cracked his head yet."

Devorah threw her head back laughing loudly. "Jealous much?"

"Woman, please. You know I got you sprung."

Devorah stopped laughing and sat back in her seat. Eyes narrowed, lips pursed and ready to fire off venom I was sure, she remained silent just ice grilling me. *Here we go.* We sat there in uncomfortable silence for a few minutes before Devorah let out a low chuckle.

"You think you got me on lock, huh?"

A cocky smirk spread over my face before I answered. "Don't think; know."

"And you're sure of that, huh?"

Something in her tone let me know that I should probably be a little less cocky with this answer. She was giving me a chance to amend. The truth was I didn't know how she felt about me. We'd been dating...or whatever the hell you could call alternating spending time at either of our houses for the past couple months. She took that silly ass pledge I made up, but that meant nothing. She was adequately demonstrative or whatever, but the fact that we were rarely around anyone else but each other gave me no clue about how she really felt about me. I'd already put my balls in her purse by agreeing to this no outside dates within a twenty mile radius shit, so I was not about to ask her to talk about her feelings.

"I mean..." I trailed off, shrugging, "You're a hard nut to crack, but you ain't put me out yet, so I gotta chalk this one up to the sprung column."

Devorah laughed, "I'm fucking with you, El."

I nodded, "Yep, that's what I thought. Sprung."

Devorah laughed as we finished up our meal and departed ways. We initially had plans to meet up after work, but part of the reason I had surprised her for lunch was because I needed to break our evening plans. Trey called me earlier, throwing up the SOS. He didn't want to get into it over the phone, but something told me there was trouble in paradise. Bee and I weren't going to be doing much besides being laid up and catching a flick, so rescheduling wasn't a huge deal.

———

"So you just gonna sit here, drinking my beer and taking

up space in my house, or are you gonna tell me what was so important that I cancelled on my girl tonight?"

Trey came over and had been acting strange since he arrived. He kept one hand in his pocket and got up intermittently to pace my living room. In the ten minutes since he'd been here, he hadn't said a word. I was being patient, letting him cook, but now I was annoyed. I sat back, sipping my beer waiting for him to finally say something. He stopped pacing, took that damn hand out his pocket and sat a small blue box on the end table in front of me.

"Is that…"

"Yep."

"Are you…"

"Yep."

"So can I say it?"

Trey cut his eyes over to me, a look of exasperation on his face. "You think that's what I wanna hear right now?"

"You think I give a fuck about what you wanna hear when I'm right?"

"Man, whatever. So get this shit though, I went to ask her dad for his permission and do you know this motherfucker said no."

"Wait. I thought you and Walt were on good terms?"

"Me too. But when you've kept his daughter on hold for damn near fifteen years, those good terms lose some of their luster. I mean he's never been rude, but man, I didn't think he'd straight up tell me no."

"So what you gonna do?"

"I'm going to ask her anyway," Trey responded and then ran down his plan to me.

"That's pretty ballsy, bruh. But wait…you tryna do all this shit by when?"

"I got three days. Which is why I need your help. I've

talked to her sister Tracee and managed to get them on a flight. Putting them up at the Omni for the night, but I need you to bring them to Pembroke for the engagement surprise."

"You got it, man. So how you feel?"

"Nervous as fuck."

"So what made you break down?"

"Pregnancy."

"Wait...Demi is..."

"Nah, man, but we thought she might be. That shit had me shook. She told me that if she was pregnant the baby wasn't going to have my name despite us being together. Because why is it important that the baby have my name when its mother didn't? Said it would be coming from her body, she'd be the primary caregiver, so why shouldn't it have her name, too?"

"Yikes."

"Yep. Fucked me right on up. So I thought about the reason I was so opposed to marrying Demi and honestly, I couldn't even remember why the fuck I started this no marriage BS."

"It was because--"

"Nigga, I don't need your reminder. Moral of the story is that's dead."

"So you really are going all in, huh?"

A grin broke out over Trey's face.

"For broke."

"Aw shit! Congrats, bruh. You think she's going to say yes?"

"You think she ain't?!"

We both laughed at that. I couldn't believe my boy had finally come to his senses. I mean damn, the brother was damn near married already since he and Demi had been inseparable since college. His parents' marriage imploding during our senior year really did a number on him though. Before all of that went down, he talked nonstop about marrying Demi and keeping her pregnant with a gang of kids. Glad to see he'd worked through whatever shit was lingering and was concentrating on making his girl happy.

DEVORAH

"I saw Sophie the other day. That baby is so adorable. She'd be cuter if she were made of half of you though. You just had to give Everett away to that lil red girl. Now look at you, lonely as you wanna be," my mother laughed.

We had been on the phone for the past twenty minutes and I wondered how long it would take her to work in a reference to the fact that I was still single. This was part of the reason that despite us living only a few minutes apart, I refused to visit her in person more often. We did dinner once a week if she was lucky and that was it. She still, however, insisted on calling me daily much to my chagrin. And in every damn conversation, she found some kind of way to bring up the fact that I was, as she calls it "alone and lonely".

"Takes one to know one, Lonely Linda," I joked.

"Watch your mouth lil girl. Been there; done that. I've had the husband. Got the baby. You, on the other hand, can barely manage to hold onto a boyfriend for more than six months."

"By choice..."

"Mmmhmmm, so you say. You sure there isn't anything you want to tell me. I may not understand it, but Mama is always here for you no matter what."

"Ma, what are you talking about?"

"Maybe you got a lil girlfriend instead of a boyfriend? I'm not judging you..."

"Oh God, Ma! I'm not a lesbian. I'd tell you if I were."

It'd certainly make my life a helluva lot easier right now.

"You sure, baby? I mean it has been a while since you brought a young man around. I'd love you regardless, you know that, right? Retha's girl came out the cupboard recently and nobody looks at her any differently."

"Out the closet, mama. And Jenice wasn't ever *in* a closet to begin with."

"Cupboard, closet...wherever. It's a storage space. And I just want you to know that I won't mind if you're a secret lesbian. Just make sure she makes enough that we can buy me some grandbabies."

"Ma! I'm not a secret lesbian. I'm actually seeing someone. A male someone."

"Mmmhmmm, sure baby."

"I am!"

"When you bringing him by to meet your mama?"

"No time soon and you know why..."

"Aw. C'mon, Devvy. You must cut mama some slack on that one. You told me y'all were a sure thing. How was I supposed to know the boy couldn't stand a couple few questions?"

The last man I'd seriously considered serious relationship material, Mark, was to whom she was referring. He and I had been dating monogamously for about six months when he asked about meeting my mother. I wasn't too keen on the idea, but he had it in his mind that we needed to go to "the next level" and in order for that to happen, he had to meet my mother. We planned to have brunch at her place after church. Church wasn't really my thing, but she somehow convinced me that she needed to see how Mark "comported himself in the house of the Lord", so church it was. Because he was a good sport, Mark went along with it. We met my mother for an early service and then headed to her house to chow down on the brunch spread she had awaiting us.

We were having a good time, or so I thought, eating and making pleasant conversation. Mark entertained my mother's off-color commentary about the pastor's wife's new wig and various other inappropriate comments about random church members. At some point, conversation turned to more personal questions about Mark and his familial history. She started off innocently enough, but soon crossed the line into asking preposterous questions about his virility and how soon he wanted to knock me up. Mark handled himself well for the most part, but when she asked if he had any nuts in his family tree—he left abruptly.

I later found out that his mother was actually in a mental health institution, dealing with issues related to bipolar disorder and schizophrenia that left her vacillating between manic peaks and ocean deeps lulls. My mother's ten-minute rant about "Looney Lucy" from her old neighborhood did me no favors. Turns out that was Mark's mom. Needless to say, I was cool on bringing anyone else around Mama anytime soon. Not that I was bringing Ellis around her soon anyway. I could see it now; she'd be calling me all sorts of harlots and jezebels for "knowing both of Randi's boys biblically". I didn't want or need that kind of stress in my life.

"Ma. C'mon. You know good and well a couple questions weren't why Mark dumped me."

"I'm sure your little attitude had something to do with it as well," she trailed off.

"Nope, not doing this with you. Love you, mama. Talk to you later."

I hung up the phone knowing that she'd call me back immediately. Sure enough, my phone rang instantly, flashing her face across the screen wearing her favorite Sunday go to meeting hat.

"I don't know where you get this rudeness from. Must be your daddy's side of the family."

"You called me back to—"

"I called you back to say I love you too, lil miss rudeness," my mother said and immediately clicked off the line.

Laughing, I placed my phone back on the charging station on my breakfast bar and continued cleaning the kitchen. Cadence was supposed to be coming by later. She and Geoff had an obstetrician appointment today to find out the sex of the baby. Ellis and I had a bet on the sex of the baby that I was desperate to win because it meant he'd have to cook my favorite meal that he prepares—his gumbo. I didn't know who taught that man how to make a roux, but it was the basis for a ridiculously addictive dish. It was almost comparable to some of the gumbo I had on that trip to NOLA for AdTech that started this whole damn shebang.

That seemed like a lifetime ago. I couldn't believe that Ellis and I were still...dating. *If you wanted to call it that.* Honestly, I couldn't believe he stuck around with my ridiculousness for this long. I was sure he'd be bored of me now and moving along to the next flavor, while I mended my broken heart, but nope. He'd been hanging in here patiently. Cade said that I should trust his intentions, but I still didn't know. It'd only been a few months of us seriously trying to be together. If I gave in, the thrill of the chase would be gone with him right behind it I'm sure.

———

"So remember when were at Cluck and I told you to trust my mother's intuition? In ya face, sucka!"

Cadence barely made it through the door before thrusting the sonogram photo in my face.

"Sis, what am I supposed to be seeing in this Rorschach blot? You wanna hold your hands still, perhaps?"

"Your niece, heffa!" Cadence said, snatching the photo back.

"You're having a girl?"

"Yes, Devorah. Keep up. I told you this *weeks* ago."

"Your faulty intuition also tried to convince me that Ellis and I were meant to be and that yet remains to be seen, so..."

Cadence rolled her eyes as she strolled past me toward the kitchen. I closed the door that she'd left wide open and walked into the kitchen to see her rooting through my fridge.

"Sis, where is the food? I know you've got to be eating well. It certainly looks like it from here. And I know El doesn't play that eating out every day shit you're normally on..."

Did this heffa just call me fat?

"And who's to say he's here every day?"

Cadence turned from the fridge and leveled me with an amused look.

"Don't get cute."

She pointed to my breakfast bar, where a charger was still in the plug.

"Android charger, when you're a slave to the Cult of Jobs. Size 13 Js near the doorway aren't yours unless your feet have had a sudden growth spurt in your thirties. And finally, this damn craft beer I see in your fridge when you don't even drink beer like that. Bet if I went into your bedroom his draws have their own drawer and there's a soft bristled toothbrush in the holder next to yours in the en suite. So…"

"En suite? Really, Cade. You've been watching too much HGTV."

"And you aren't a masterful seguer, so…like I said… where's the food?"

"Seguer?" I said, arching a brow.

Cadence walked over to the cabinet, grabbing a glass to fill with water from the refrigerator. She said something I couldn't hear over the whirr of the ice machine, so I asked her to repeat herself.

"I said…sis, you're the wordsmith working in advertis ing. You sure that ain't a word?"

She walked over to the kitchen table, sitting down, looking at the sonogram picture again.

"I'm a graphic designer, I don't even do words and I know that ain't a goddamn word."

"Stop taking God's name in vain in front of my baby, you heathen. Seriously though, Bee, what's up with that food, though? How do you invite me over here and not have anything for me and my child to snack on?"

"A—you invited yourself over here. And two, there's fruit in the crisper."

"Devorah, you think I can see down that low?"

Cadence deadpanned.

"Sis, you're not that pregnant. Cut it out. We haven't had a chance to go food shopping this week. It's been kinda hectic with the engagement and everything," I said, purposefully timing my statement with Cade's sip of water.

She sputtered, nearly spitting water all over my table before catching herself. I tried holding back laughter as she gathered her composure, but failed.

"En-who-ment now?"

Still laughing, I replied, "Trey and Demi got engaged the other day. Ellis helped Trey set up the surprise and had been running around with him all week in preparation."

"I was about to be hot if you suckas got engaged and I wasn't included. I'm the reason y'all are even together!"

Just then my phone rang. I walked over to the counter to see who was calling and saw Celena's sunny smile flashing across the screen. I immediately swiped to answer it.

"Hey, boo."

"Hey chick, what you up to today?"

"Not much, Cade just came by with the sonogram results. We're chillin'. Likely gonna order in some food depending on her damn cravings."

Cadence piped up, "Who the hell you giving my life story to on the phone over there?"

"It's Celena, calm down."

"CellyCel, your friend is stressing me out," Cade called out in the background.

I switched the phone to speaker so Cade wouldn't have to keep yelling like we were in a damn barn somewhere and walked back toward the table where she was sitting.

"Y'all having bestie time or can I intrude?" Celena asked.

I rolled my eyes at the question, as Celena was a welcomed figure in our friend circle on many occasions. Hell, there were times when those two got together without me to do their whole sportsball thing. Both of them were avid basketball fans whereas I could take or leave it. They got frustrated with me pointing out who I thought was cute instead of being focused whatever ball needed to go in what hole.

"Girl, if you don't bring your ass over here. Preferably with a gyro with extra tzatziki sauce from *Opa*! Ooh and those butter garlic fries. Ooh and a chocolate shake, extra thick."

I laughed at Cade's fat ass antics and chimed in, "Come on through."

"You want food, too?" Celena asked.

"Sure. You can bring me the same as Cade, sans the shake."

"Aight, see y'all in a bit."

"Bye, babe."

An impromptu girls night was overdue. Ellis monopolized a lot of my time these days and I'd been neglecting my friends. I mean, I saw Celena at work daily, but we hadn't really had the time to catch up with everything that's been happening over the last few weeks. I knew she was still reeling from the JP situation and that bleeding over into her professional life. Work had been extremely stressful; with Tom openly critiquing Celena at every juncture as if it were her fault that Jake's raggedy ass played us. I knew for a fact that she never let their relationship affect her quality of work nor did she treat Parker & Associates any different than any other high revenue client we had. The blame for us losing that account lay squarely on the shoulders of that cowardly ass Jake Parker and no one else.

———

"So when are you gonna finally let him take you outside within a fifty mile radius? Or you still scared of your mama?" Celena asked.

She'd arrived a little over half an hour ago. She and Cade had been drilling me nonstop about Ellis since she'd arrived. Perhaps inviting her over wasn't such a great idea. Not if these two heffas kept on putting me under the hot lights of interrogation.

"We do go outside."

"Picnics in either of your backyards don't count, sis."

"We got coffee the other day. At Starbucks. Together. Outside."

"Yep and he told me that as soon as he tried to hold your hand, you freaked the fuck out," Cadence piped up.

I rolled my eyes at her. I'd been trying, but with so much of our family living in the immediate area as well as their large network of friends; it was difficult for me to completely give in. The last thing I needed was the news of Ellis and I being together to get back to "the grownups" before I could find a way to bring it to them myself.

"He can take me outside in town with PDA as soon as you admit to your little crush on Josh in IT."

Celena quickly averted her gaze. I'd had a hunch about her feelings, but this reaction just confirmed it. I noticed he was in her office fairly often and she'd just gotten a brand new MacBook Air; so I knew it didn't have nothing to do with troubleshooting.

"Damn CellyCel with the quick bounce back! Who's Josh?" Cadence crowed.

"Joshua is...a friend," Celena replied, still blushing, "But who he is ain't got nothing to do with the fact that you're treating your main like a side, Devvy. Don't try to deflect!"

Just as I was about to reply to her, my text tone went off. I got up to retrieve my phone from the kitchen and left Cadence teasing Celena. Picking up the phone, I saw it was a message from El. It was a link to a video on YouTube. He had taken to sending me a link daily, with a movie trailer he said reminded him of me or us. During all of our Netflix & Chillesque dates, I feel like we'd watched every cheesy ass romantic comedy out there. And not by *my* choice. Quiet as kept, Ellis had a serious romcom addiction. Anything starring Sanaa Lathan, Nia Long, or Jennifer Lopez and he was all in. At first I thought he was only into the movies because of the fine female costars, but he knew these damn movies line for line. Even those low budget, straight to DVD films. We'd seen them all...good, bad & ugly. As cheesy as it was, I actually began to look forward to the trailers every day. Who knew he was a big old manwhore softy? Certainly not me.

Brown Sugar? Seriously?

You denying the cinematic greatness of Taye Diggs and fine ass Sanaa Lathan? — Baellis

Gotta be two greatnesses…

So I guess me telling you you're the perfect verse over a tight beat won't get you wet? — Baellis

I don't like you right now.

What about, "you're my air"? All the sistas in the theater lost their minds when Taye said it. — Baellis

;-* — Baellis

What the hell is this face?

"Cade...what's a winky face with an asterisk mean?" I asked, strolling back into the den where Cadence and Celena were deep in conversation. They quickly stopped talking as I walked back into the room, something I'd bring up later on. For now I needed to know what the hell this face was.

"What are you talking about?"

"This," I said, thrusting my phone in her direction.

She quickly glanced at it and said, "Oh. Girl, that's a kissy face. What are you seventy-two? How do you not know emoticons? You were on AIM with the rest of us in the late 90s, right?"

"Now you know my mama thought the internet was a tool of Satan. Why is your friend stuck in the days of dialup?"

"That's your man."

"He is not—"

"Don't finish that lie. I want my baby to make it out of the womb and not killed by way of the lightning strike that's sure to follow such a bold faced lie."

I rolled my eyes and flopped down on the sofa between Cadence and Celena.

"Anyway. You know him better than I do."

Cadence shrugged, "The better question is why does he refuse to use emoji like he doesn't have a phone equipped with them?"

"Actually the best question is...Baellis? Really, friend?" Celena laughed.

"For the record, he did that shit. *Not* me."

"Sure, friend."

8

ELLIS

I sat in my car in Devorah's driveway for a few minutes before getting out. I had come up with a game plan. Now all I had to do was convince her to go along with it. I got out of the car and before I made it fully up to the walkway, her door opened.

"Hey, pretty."

She blushed at the compliment.

"Hi, you."

I walked into the house, hauling her against me as I shut the door.

"And how are you tonight?" I asked, pressing her back into the door as I leaned in for a kiss.

Not waiting for an answer, I lowered my mouth to hers. I pressed a series of soft kisses to her mouth before nibbling on her bottom lip, drawing it into my mouth. She gasped softly, her mouth opening just enough for me to slip my tongue between her lips. Our tongues danced briefly before I tried pulling back. Bee's hands moved to the back of my head, holding me close, taking over the kiss until she got her fill. Drawing back slowly, she surveyed me with a wicked grin.

"Great, now that you're here."

"Is that right?"

Pulling her bottom lip between her teeth, she nodded.

"Come on, I have a surprise."

"Oh yeah?"

She just nodded again, grabbing my hand, and leading me to her office. She motioned for me to sit down at the computer and she sat down on my lap.

I nuzzled her neck and said, "Oh, I like this surprise already."

She giggled and opened the lid of her MacBook. When it opened and I saw what she had been looking at I stayed quiet. She had been looking at a website advertising flights to New Orleans at a ridiculously low price.

"So. I was thinking. I know you're being incredibly patient with me about this whole no local outside dates thing. I realize I'm being utterly ridiculous, so I want to propose a compromise."

She went on to tell me how she has been looking at getaways for us and how this NOLA one crossed her desk earlier today and she saw it as a sign that maybe we should take a trip together. She rambled on and on until I began laughing.

"What's so funny?"

"I think we spend too much time together."

"What?" she huffed and tried scrambling off my lap.

I held her firmly in place as I tried to explain. "Hold on, hold on...don't you even try it. Let me finish."

She stopped struggling against my hold, but remained silent. I reached into my pocket and handed her my phone.

I had an email application open with the deals from that same airline. I had come over here with the idea of whisking her away for a date since I couldn't get her to go out with me here. I knew she had no rebuttal to turn down a date hundreds of miles away from where anyone knew us.

Looking at the phone, a small grin spread across her face.

"So I guess we're NOLA bound?"

"Not quite..." I trailed off and filled her in on Trey and Demi planning their Vegas elopement.

"So Sin City, then?"

"Just say the word and we're booked, baby."

"Welp, since y'all stole Parker and Associates from us, my calendar is wide open."

I chuckled, raising a brow. "Stole? Jake Parker came to us, practically begging for us to take them on. My team was actually focused on their competitor before Jake met with Eric and the senior management team."

Shifting in my lap, Bee turned so that she was fully facing me. "Wait. *Jake* was the one who came to y'all? Not Senior or Junior?"

I shrugged. "Yep. Something about needing to make a clean break."

"That motherfucker!"

Bee leapt from my lap, pacing back and forth mumbling about throwing hands. I got up, grabbing her forearms to get her attention.

"Baby. Calm down. What's going on?"

"Ol raggedy ass Carlton Banks lookin' ass nigga. Tryna play my friend. Got his good damn nerve. I will fuck his shit all the way up."

She shook off my hands, moving out of the office and back into the living room area. When I walked into the room she was rifling through her bag in search of something. Frustrated with not being able to find it upon first glance, she overturned the bag, dumping everything out onto the couch. Whatever she was looking for was clearly not in the bag as she stalked out of the room and into the kitchen. She came back into the living room a few minutes later, clutching her phone in her hands, still visibly upset. I sat there quietly, not sure why what I'd said had set her off. She sat down on my lap, burrowing her face into my shoulder. Instantly, I wrapped my arms around her, rubbing her back in soothing circles. She murmured something into my chest that I barely understood.

"Come again?" I said, shifting so we were eye to eye.

"If you want to end this, please promise me you won't ever pull this ghosting shit."

She blew out a breath, looking down, fidgeting with her hands.

"Babe. Look at me," I said, tilting her chin up so I could see her face.

Her eyes were reddened, full of unshed tears. Leaning in, I gave her a gentle kiss on the lips. She heaved a sigh.

"Just promise me you won't disappear..."

"I'm not going anywhere, baby. If I was, you'd be the first to know."

She stared at me for moments, eyes searching my face. My answer and whatever she saw in my eyes seemed to satisfy her. She settled back against my chest and then began talking. The story she told me was one of the most nonsensical tales I'd ever heard.

———

"Roger, you got a minute?"

Roger was my counterpart on the national sales team and my backup whenever I needed to be out of the office. He was this white cat, who swore he was down for the cause. Dated sistas, stayed at the local juke joints, and had a propensity for calling everybody "my man". I rarely gave him static because he was a good dude deep down, just tried a little too hard to come off as down.

"What up, E?"

"Can you cover Parker for me until I get back?"

"It's nothing, my man, you know I got you. How long will you be gone?"

"I just need you to hold it down from Friday through Monday. Robert Junior and Jake are supposed to be coming in for an update Friday afternoon. Pauline has a general idea of all of the information they'll be looking for, so she can get you up to speed before they come. Thanks, man. I appreciate it."

"It's just what we do, bruh," Roger said, holding out one fist for a pound, "A brotha's gotta make sure somebody is here to watch his back, know what I'm sayin'?"

"Right. Appreciate it, Rog."

I turned and left his office. I was halfway down the hall before I heard Roger calling my name. I turned back to see what he wanted.

"You just gon' leave me hanging, my man?" Roger called out.

I was certainly not walking back to his office to give him no damn fist pound. I just threw my hands up, giving him the wink and a gun gesture.

"You da man, Rog!"

Completely missing the sarcasm in my gesture coupled with those words, Roger preened and strutted back into his office. *What a clown.* I chuckled, as I made my way back to my office. My phone rang and I picked it up mid chuckle.

"Ellis Taylor."

"I need a favor."

———

"Uncle El, you said we could go to Easy Sundae..." Sophie whined as we pulled into my driveway.

"And we will, Sweetpea. I've just got to run in super quick to grab my wallet. C'mon. The faster we get it, the quicker you're face planting in a banana split."

I unlocked the doors and came around to open the door for Sophie since the child lock was on. Everett called me frantically needing someone to pick up Soph from after care. Our mom was supposed to pick her up per their usual plans, but somewhere along the way their signals got crossed and moms went on one of those old people bus trips instead of picking up her darling grandgirl. So I left work a little early to scoop the little one. And of course, since she had me wrapped around her little finger we were headed to Easy Like Sundae Morning for pre-dinner dessert when I realized that I didn't have my wallet. Since Easy Sundae was cash only I had to stop at the bank. I'd pulled into the drive-through ATM only to keep on trucking back to my house where I was sure that my wallet sat on my dresser.

"Isn't that Auntie Beebee's car?" Sophie asked, dancing along the sidewalk, while pointing across the street.

I looked over at the car that she pointed to that was parked across from my house. It looked like Bee's Malibu, but I knew she wouldn't be in this neighborhood for no reason so I didn't think anything of it.

"Nope, it's not babygirl. C'mon, so we can get inside and you can help Uncle El find his wallet so we can get ice cream."

"Nah, I'm pretty sure that's Auntie Beebee's car. Is she coming to get ice cream with us? I haven't seen Auntie Beebee in a whole lotta days."

"That's not her car, Sweetpea. Auntie Beebee is still at work. C'mon..."

I waited for Soph to run in front of me, while I fished out my keys. She skipped up the porch and easily opened the storm door, which I knew I'd locked that morning when I left. I moved Sophie aside to open my main door. As soon as the lock clicked, I could hear music playing faintly. I opened the door to see Bee standing in my foyer; hands on hips, legs splayed wearing the tiniest piece of lingerie I'd ever seen. I licked my lower lip, moving toward her when a tiny voice interrupted my dirty ass thoughts.

"See, Uncle El I *told you* Auntie Beebee was here. Auntie, were you sleeping? Why are you in your PJs?"

Just that fast I'd forgotten Sophie was there. All I saw was my girl looking good enough to eat and I was instantaneously hungry.

"Oh my God!" Bee yelled, before running down the hallway.

"Here, Soph. Sit down for a minute and watch some TV while I find my wallet so we can get ice cream."

"Fiiiiiiiine, I guess," she huffed.

"Sophia Lauren Taylor."

She instantly dropped the attitude when she heard the bass in my voice. I turned on the TV to one of those kid's stations and she plopped on the couch, entranced. As I moved to walk back toward my bedroom, Sophia called out to me.

"Uncle El?"

"Yes, Sweetpea."

"Can you please ask Auntie Beebee to hurry up and put on her clothes so we can go?"

Chuckling, I responded, "Sure thing, babygirl."

I walked into to my room to find Devorah burrowed beneath the covers. I lifted the duvet and she was curled into a ball, hands covering her face.

"Hey, pretty."

"Oh my God, El," she said, lowering her hands, "Did I scar Beanie for life?"

She looked genuinely freaked out and I couldn't help but chuckle. I leaned down and pulled the bedcovers back a little more.

"So...Soph is currently watching TV as if nothing happened so you didn't scar her, baby. And two, you need to get your ass dressed because your little niecey-pooh wants Auntie Beebee to come for ice cream, too. But uh... when we get back though..."

She looked up at me, running her tongue across her lower lip. I couldn't resist and leaned down to draw her tongue into my mouth in a lazy kiss.

"Mmmmmm, as much as I'd like to finish this, we have an impatient seven year old in there waiting on her ice cream. I'm surprised she hasn't made her way back here already asking what's taking so long."

"I heard you have to put that bass in your voice to get her in line. You plan on using that with me later?" Bee said.

It took everything in me to back away and say, "Five minutes or we're leaving without you!"

I had to leave that room before Sophia, her ice cream and anything else that wasn't Bee and her tempting form was a distant memory. Devorah dressed in record time and we set out to take Sophia to Easy Like Sundae Morning. While we were at Easy Sundae, Everett called asking if Soph could stay for dinner as well because he and Cassidy were both tied up at work longer than expected. So we ended up going back to my house and ordering a pizza— pepperoni because sausage looked too much like hamster poop according to the little miss. I knew better than to argue the issue, so as usual what the princess wanted was what the princess got. After we ate dinner, we settled in to watch a movie.

Within in ten minutes of the movie starting, Sophie had draped herself beneath her special blanket that she kept over here. Laying across both Bee and I, Sophie drifted off, snoring lightly.

"Are you staying over?" I asked Bee, making sure to keep my voice low to not wake the kid.

"That was the plan...is that cool?"

"Is putting back on that little number you had on earlier part of the plan too?"

"It can be...later."

Peering to ensure the kid was still sleeping I replied, "There's no time like the present."

"Good things come to those who wait," she drawled, the slightest hint of sleepiness creeping into her voice.

"Absolutely. Matter of fact, let me see where her parents are...I do believe I've waited long enough."

Bee giggled softly as I got up to retrieve my phone to call Everett. When I picked it up, I saw that I had a few texts from Everett waiting. Reading them, I saw that he asked me to keep Soph overnight and he'd come get her in the morning for school. That seemed a little strange, so I decided to give him a call to see what was going on. My call went unanswered, so I replied to his text letting him

know it was all good. I walked back into the den where
Bee and Sophie were to see that Bee had dozed off now,
too. I picked Sophie up, transferring her into the bed in
my spare room. Her clothes would have to do double duty
as pajamas because she had outgrown all of the spare pairs
of pajamas I kept over here when I babysat for Everett and
Cass in the past. Just as I pulled the comforter up over her,
Sophie stirred, eyes slowly opening.

"Go back to sleep, Sweetpea," I said, leaning over to
kiss her forehead.

She muttered something before her eyes drifted back
closed. I waited for a couple minutes more to ensure she
was sleeping peacefully, then left the room to go back to
Bee. When I got back in the den, the tv was off, Sophie's
blankie was put away, and Bee was nowhere in sight.

"Looking for me?" Bee said from behind me in a
honey-coated voice.

I turned around to see Bee draped across the doorway
in the flimsy lingerie from earlier.

"Now is later?" I said, advancing toward her.

Not answering, Bee simply turned and walked down
the hall toward my bedroom. I hung back to enjoy the
view. The scant lace of the underwear barely contained her
curvy backside, which jiggled a little with every step she
took. She was about halfway there when she noticed I
hadn't fallen into step behind her. Glancing over her
shoulder she asked, "You comin'?"

"Definitely. But not before you," I said, slowly strolling
the length of the hall to reach her, sweeping her into my
arms and continuing the short distance into my bedroom.

9

DEVORAH

"I didn't disturb your groove the other night, did I? I had no idea Rhett asked El to pick Bug up from school. I thought she was going to Mother Taylor's. I'm so sorry, friend," Cassidy apologized for the fourth time in our barely two minute conversation. I could barely get out an initial greeting before she apologized profusely for messing up my special night. She knew what I had planned for Ellis since she was the one who'd managed to swipe his spare key from Ev to loan to me for my night of seduction that got thrown off course.

"Oh my gosh, Cass. Like I told you when you walked in, *it was fine*. Plans were altered slightly, but all's well that ends well."

And it had certainly ended well. Several times over. Thank God the guest room that housed Sophie was far enough away to blanket the ear-piercing screams I was sure I let out that evening. I'd already scarred the baby earlier that day, God forbid her being awakened by my cries of passion that Ellis tried in vain to swallow.

"I know what you said, but I also know how much

trying to do something special for El meant to you. I'm so sorry. Again. Really. Once again my husband's lack of listening skills has come to roost."

"Stop apologizing, Cass. What's done is done."

"Whew. Ellis must've really put it on you, sis. You speaking in clichés and adages."

"I mean..."

"On second thought, don't answer that. He still is my brother-in-law and ew. I don't want to think of any part of him being sexual."

"Oh come off it, Cass. We've shared much more than that over the years. Anyway...what happened to y'all last night? I didn't know the world of accountancy was so high stakes that you had to pull all-nighters?"

Cassidy briefly flushed red and lowered her eyes.

"Ohhhhh, I see. You sent ya lil blocker my way so you could get your groove back. Ain't that a bitch?"

"No, it wasn't like that. You know I wouldn't..." Cass trailed off, her voice catching slightly, "It was an honest mistake. Actually forget that, it was Rhett's fault for once again not fucking listening when I was talking."

Whoa.

Cass wasn't a swearer. And even when she did let a bad word slip every now and again, the worst I'd heard her say was "hell" or "damn" in the nearly fifteen years that I'd known her. For her to be dropping f-bombs meant whatever was going on had to be serious. Cassidy raised her head and I recognized the sheen of unshed tears. Her eyes were red and a little puffy now that I was really taking a good look at her.

"What's going on, Cass?"

"I think I'm leaving Rhett."

"I'm sorry, what? I know I didn't hear you right..."

"No, you did. It's...we...it's for the best. Before things get really bad and start to affect Bug. Oh God, my poor baby..."

Cassidy broke down into full on sobbing and I moved over to the couch to comfort my friend. Pulling her into a hug, I rubbed her back in small, but firm circles until her crying subsided. Damn. Cass and Ev were my real life relationship goals—along with Cade and Geoff. Cheesy social media hashtag aside, I'd always been a bit envious of the easy way in which they interacted with one another. Cade and Geoff's relationship never quite compared to the legend that was *Cassett* though. Everett always seemed to be in tune with his wife's needs, catering to her every whim. She took a few deep shuddering breaths before disengaging from my embrace.

"Okay, start at the beginning."

"He's messing around on me, Dev. And you know I don't do cheaters. Not after seeing my mom dogged out by my dad for all those years."

"Everett James 'Solid as a rock do-gooder Boy Scout ass' Taylor is doing what now?"

"Fucking around. Putting *my dick* in holes it doesn't belong."

My jaw dropped. Okay, I'd seriously never seen this side of Cassidy.

"Oh my God, I'm so sorry, Cass. This is...what?"

I couldn't even form a coherent thought. Everett had always been the most dependable guy I'vd known; loyal to a fault. Wrapped up in Ellis, I hadn't seen he and Cass that much lately, but everything seemed to be fine at Sophie's recital, which was the last time I could remember being in their presence together for more than a couple minutes at a time. Come to think of it, he did look rather bedraggled when he came to retrieve Soph from Ellis' house that day. I'd attributed it to not getting much sleep, since I had remembered Ellis saying something about Ev working long hours developing a new game.

"What do you need me to do? You know these hands are on demand."

A brief chuckle escaped Cassidy. We sat there for a few moments in silence before she spoke again.

"When did I stop being enough?"

She sounded utterly defeated, her voice breaking on that last word.

Sighing, I responded, "I can't answer that, Cassie. But you know what I can say? Everett is an asshole. Nah, scratch that. He's a whole ass. You don't deserve to be treated this way. I hope you put his raggedy ass out and he's couch surfing at his mama's house. Or...better yet, I'm hoping Auntie Randi wouldn't let his ass in and he's hemorrhaging money at some shitty hotel with PBS as its only station...because fuck him."

"Hey! I like PBS."

"Really, Cass? That's the sticking point here? How is my niece? Does she know?"

"I told her Daddy and Mommy needed a vacation from each other. Other than being a pain in my ass about why we couldn't be the ones to stay in a hotel and have fun, she's fine. I think I've put up a good front."

"Shit, Cass."

"I know. It's a big fucking mess."

"What does he even have to say for himself?"

"Not a thing. Hell, the reason you guys got stuck with Bug the other day was because I couldn't get him to answer one question. He just kept saying 'I fucked up' whenever I pressed for details. If I just knew why, maybe this wouldn't hurt so bad."

———

"Flight attendants prepare for take off," the captain droned.

We were seated in the last row of the plane, much to my annoyance. I absolutely hated having to wait to deplane once reaching my destination. Usually when I travelled it was covered by work; so business class was almost always the option. That was the life – early boarding, free booze and legroom. Ellis was definitely more than accustomed to traveling in style, so why he purposefully chose de jure segregation was beyond me. I was already a little cranky because the flight was a red eye, so we were taking off hella late.

Flight attendants were coming through to do their final checks, so I stowed my purse below the seat and pulled my blanket tighter around me. Damn back of the plane had the nerve to feel like the Antarctic.

"You willing to share?" Ellis asked, tugging on the loose end of the blanket.

"Hell no! Shoulda brought your own. You put us in this frozen tundra!"

"Wow, really? That's how you feel?"

"YES."

I leaned over him to watch my favorite part of flying. Since Ellis refused to give me the window seat, I was draped all over him, basically. No other feeling came close to the way I felt as the plane pitched down the runway and ascended into the inky, starless black sky. I'd been on countless flights through the years and it still gave me that fluttery feeling of excitement on every ascent. Looking down upon the city lights twinkling and buildings being dwarfed in mere seconds always put me in a contemplative space. Made me a little less self-centered to realize I was only a very small part of the universe.

I leaned back to see Ellis watching me, bemused.

"What?"

"You are so goddamn gorgeous, you know that?"

I melted immediately. All of that previous annoyance dissipated with a simple ass compliment. Who in the hell was I now? *A woman in love*, the voice in my head instantly replied. Which, to be honest, scared the shit out of me. Ellis and I had yet to say those words, but I felt good about us. And where we were headed. Not so sure when it happened, but here I was, going all in. I lifted the armrest between our seats to snuggle a little closer to Ellis. He brought his arm around me instantly, drawing me in for a kiss.

"So you know what I was thinkin'?" he murmured against my lips.

"Let me call the flight attendant to see if there are any business class seats left?"

"No," he rumbled on a soft chuckle, "I was thinking about making you a four star general."

"Come again?"

"Wanted to give you some frequent flier miles."

"El, what?"

"You know...mile high..." he trailed off.

"Oh...you tryna fuck?" I smirked, "Why didn't you just say that?"

"Must you be so crass?"

"Says the man trying to induct me into the mile high

club. Which, for the record, I've been a long standing member of..."

In the faint light of the darkened plane, I saw Ellis' jaw drop.

"Word?"

"Word."

"Well damn. I guess you'll be the one making me a general tonight."

"Wait. You've never..."

"No. I was saving myself for someone special," he deadpanned.

A loud clap of laughter erupted from my mouth quicker than I could smother it with my hand.

"Wait. Is that why in the hell you got us back here like we're living in pre-Rosa times?"

"Well when I Googled..."

I broke out into giggles again. The look on Ellis' face let me know that he was less than amused.

"Awww, babe. Sorry. But that's so cute. You Googled it?"

"Not everyone is a subject matter expert at fucking more than thirty thousand feet above ground, Bee. Anyway, a number of articles suggested starting a fake fight, then making up in the bathroom, but I nixed that shit immediately because I know you're a germaphobe. Finally stumbled on one that told me to book a red eye with window and aisle seats. Wear loose fitting clothing for easy access. And to bring my own blanket because the ones provided by the airline are laced in The Clap. I knew your ass was like Linus and would have the blanket covered, so I just had to take care of everything else."

I looked up at his face and he looked so pleased with

himself. Cocky little grin, chest a lil poked out. It was so cute, I wanted to laugh again but I held it in.

"That's why you were so insistent on me wearing this damn dress."

We'd almost gotten into a huge argument right before leaving to go to the airport. We went back and forth for about fifteen minutes with him trying to get me to wear this damned dress.

I was freshly showered and ready to slip into my comfy and fashionable Ivy Park ensemble when Ellis came over to me with one of my favorite dresses in hand.

"Wear this..."

"El, you know I like to be comfortable when I travel."

"Exactly. You always talk about how comfortable this dress is whenever you wear it. And it has those pockets you're consistently amazed by. Like garments haven't had pockets for a century at the very least."

"But dresses rarely have pockets! It's a treat!"

"Bee, focus. The dress, wear it," Ellis said, trading the soft joggers I had in my hand for the dress, "You can wear your Beyoncé gear on the way home."

"So you want to just keep talkin' bout it or...?" he trailed off, raising a brow.

I moved back to the aisle seat, pulling my blanket tighter around me. Ellis' demeanor shifted immediately.

"All of your Googling didn't tell you to wait until after beverage service?" I said, winking.

"Nah, but I guess I'll defer to the expert here. Anything else I should know?"

I launched into a long explanation about logistics concerning how to pull this off, timing, and so forth. Ellis' face, as I explained what we needed to do in order to be successful at actually fucking in flight, morphed from slightly impressed to pensive with the more details I revealed.

"Exactly how many times have...wait, never mind. I don't think I want to know that."

"Just once."

"Yeah right."

"For real."

"You who said, and I quote, you were 'a longstanding member of the club' and giggled her way through my Google research tales have only done it once? I'm not buying it."

"It's the truth. And it wasn't very good, honestly. So...I mean, if we do this, you're going to have to make it worthwhile."

A cocky grin spread across Ellis' features as my words sank in.

"Challenge accepted. Now come here."

"They haven't even begun beverage service. Easy, tiger."

"Okay."

That easy acquiescence from Ellis seemed odd, so I searched his face for any signs of anger or annoyance or disappointment. None were there, just his normal resting facial expression. So I grabbed my tablet out of my bag to get back into the book I was reading until it was go time. Celena had recommended it to me. It was about three good girlfriends and their lives, set in Atlanta. I was just about halfway through, really wanted to wring the neck of one of the main characters, but the writing was so compelling I hated to put it down. I was hoping to finish it on this flight since I had more than a few hours of uninter-rupted time to really dig my heels in.

A few minutes into my reading, I felt Ellis shift into

the middle seat. I tried my best to act like I didn't feel his gaze on me and kept reading about Renee, Debra and Maxine until I felt the bottom of my blanket slowly rising. It was then that I turned to see Ellis staring with the same calm expression from before. I could normally read his thoughts from his facial expression, but he'd schooled his features into a blank slate. Still saying nothing, he shifted the blanket halfway onto his lap, and then placed his hands on both sides of my waist, scooting me in between his legs. I paused reading, twisting to look at him.

"Keep reading. I just want you close."

With the closeness of the seats and his height, our current position could not have been comfortable for him, but I was not even going to start any fuss. He wanted me close; I'd stay close. I heard the flight attendants coming down the aisle for beverage service at the same time Ellis moved his left hand from where it had been perched at my side, to slowly inching up the bottom of my dress.

His mouth pressed against my ear as he asked, "So what is your book about?"

I felt his hand creeping along my thigh as he pulled up the dress; a feather light touch he knew would drive me crazy. I shifted, trying to readjust my dress as his right hand encircled my waist, restricting my movements.

"What are you...*mmmmmmm*."

"Shhhhhhh," he breathed against my ear, "Keep reading."

My earlier shift had allowed just enough room for him to plunge two fingers into me as he slowly pumped them in and out. His thumb circled my clit, flicking it at the top of every rotation. I bit down on my lip hard, as a fluttery sensation built in my core. I could hear the flight attendants getting closer, but Ellis kept his fingers moving at a maddeningly slow pace. I felt an orgasm building when suddenly Ellis stilled his fingers. I looked up to see a flight attendant in the aisle in front of us, taking drink orders. I looked back at Ellis over my shoulder and the earlier blank look had been replaced with a devious smile. As the beverage cart bumped and rolled closer to our row, his fingers began moving again at that same deliciously torturous slow pace.

"Sir, can I get you anything?" the flight attendant asked.

Pressing down on my clit and speeding up his rotations, Ellis calmly replied that he was fine and had everything he needed.

"Miss, would you like anything to drink?" she asked me, as I clenched my thighs to still Ellis fingers that were still gently pumping. That movement didn't still his thumb, however, and I barely eked out a negative reply as I felt myself dangerously close to peaking. Ellis felt the quickening and stilled his hand movements once again.

"What are you doing to me?" I whispered.

"Just tryna make sure you're ready when it's go time," he replied, moving his hands from between my legs.

Okay...two could play this game. I shifted out of his lap, slightly maneuvering so that I could slip my hand down the front of his sweatpants. He was already hard and ready, letting out a low groan as I slipped my hand into his boxers and swiped my thumb over the head of his dick as I stroked from base to tip.

"Ain't as much fun when the rabbit's got the gun, huh?" I chuckled.

Instead of replying, Ellis removed my hand from his dick and pulled my face close to his for a kiss. So caught up in our tongues parrying for dominance, I didn't notice that Ellis had maneuvered my body to receive him until I felt the head of his dick at my slickened entrance. He teased both sets of my lips before slowly sliding inside of me, eliciting a moan that he quickly swallowed. My hips moved of their own volition, in quick, incremental thrusts as Ellis' hands traveled up my torso to palm my breasts. He played and plucked until my nipples were budded, primed and ready for this mouth. He released my lips long enough to swipe at one distended bud through the fabric of my dress. I bit down on my lip, grinding onto him a bit harder as I tried to stifle a whimper as he went back and forth between my breasts.

I felt my orgasm building, cresting as he pulled my hips closer, thrusting up slightly and grinding his pelvis against mine. As the base of his shaft came into contact with my clit, I lost it. Ellis quickly reacted, covering my mouth with his as he muffled the satisfied yelp of passion I released as I came. Moments later his climax followed. The necessity of breathing caused him to pull back a bit and we stared at each other, chests moving in opposition as we struggled to regain our breaths.

"That was..." I whispered, trailing off because I had no words to describe it.

I felt his dick twitch inside of me and instinctively ground my hips against his once again.

"Dangerous," he finally replied, stilling my movements. "You make me forget myself. And condoms far too often."

"You started this, you know, Mr. Mile High Seduction."

"And you upped the ante when I realized you weren't wearing panties."

"Touché."

We disengaged, each heading to opposite lavatories to clean ourselves up as best as one could on an airplane before reconvening at our seats. We settled back into a loose embrace and I dozed off, fully satiated with no thoughts of finishing the book that had me so completely captivated before.

We'd planned on arriving in Vegas in advance of everyone else to have a little time to ourselves before being thrust into The Trey and Demi Show. Ellis was in charge of all of the arrangements, so I was pleasantly surprised when our hired car pulled up into the semi-circle entrance of The Drake Hotel & Casino. The Drake was one in a franchise of several hotels known for their exquisite amenities and sumptuous suites. I'd mentioned to Ellis in passing that I wanted to stay at one of their properties after reading about the family that owned and operated the hotels and being pleasantly surprised at it being a Black family—two brothers and a sister at the helm.

Despite being El Cheapo with our flights, El spared no expense when it came to the room. The suite was ridiculously large, but I was so damned tired the only thing I care about was face planting into a bed and soon. Knowing I would regret not doing it, I quickly washed my face before donning pajamas and snuggling under the covers. I had no idea what else Ellis had planned for us, but I couldn't wait to see what the rest of this trip had in store.

10

ELLIS

"This shower is definitely big enough for hella activities," were the first words I heard as I turned over in bed, turning off the alarm I'd set. Bee didn't realize that the part of the bathroom she was in lacked a door and her whispered words carried further than intended. Whoever she was talking to, likely CadyMac, must've said something scandalous in reply because all I heard after that was an incredulous gasp and high pitched giggles. Which was all right with me because a laughing Bee was the best Bee. I glanced over at the clock and saw it was barely six a.m., but there was no telling how long Bee had actually been awake.

I remember her mentioning her internal clock going haywire at the reality of traveling back in time that going west always provided. We had a pretty full day today. I planned a few surprises for her in the morning and afternoon and then we were going our separate ways in the evening to partake in the bachelor and bachelorette parties. I had no idea what the ladies had planned, but I had a very low-key night lined up for Trey. The only directive I had been given was no strippers. I felt like this came more from Demi than Trey, but I knew I would have to respect the boundary or hear about the shit later. I knew better than to get on Demi's bad side, so the night I planned was going to be rather tame; no *Hangover* antics. Since my boss had an in with the manager of the Drake, I was able to procure a private gambling room for us all night, with an unlimited top-shelf bar and access to the premium cigar lounge.

Before that though? Quality time with my lady. Our first activity of the day was scheduled for seven a.m., so I needed get out of bed to shower soon before we headed out for the day. Bee was a bit of an adrenaline junkie, so I had found a couple things for us to do today that would feed her addiction. I wanted to make our first real date one to remember. After we finished all of the crazy shit, I scheduled a couple's massage for us since Bee was complaining about being tense due to some friction and recent unrest at work. I wasn't too keen about some dude having his hands all over her, but sometimes you had to be a little uncomfortable for the woman you love. Besides he only had sixty minutes and restricted areas, I had the rest of our lives with no restrictions.

Just as I swung my legs out of bed, Bee walked back into the bedroom. She looked freshly showered; with damp hair wearing the Ivy Park gear I'd made her discard last night.

"Hi," she said, softly.

"Hey."

"Good morning."

"Morning. Jury is out on how good it is though."

"Oh," she said, arching one brow.

"Come here."

She took her time rounding the bed to come stand in front of me. As soon as she was in arm's reach, I pulled her down into my lap, nuzzling and nibbling her neck slightly. Bee giggled and tried pulling back, but I banded my arms tighter around her and kept feasting.

"That make the morning better for you?"

"It's a start. You ready for today?"

"I'm all showered and set to go, but I would be better prepared if you'd tell me what we're doing and why we needed to be up so damn early."

"You trust me?"

There was a slight hesitation before she answered, "I do."

"Then that's all you need to know for now."

With one last lingering kiss, I set her aside on the bed and made my way to the bathroom. She was quick on my heels, but silent. I walked toward the glass-enclosed shower and started the spray. I could feel Bee's glare on me as I undressed and stepped into the shower. She sat just outside the shower, on the bench of the vanity looking at me as I showered.

"You got money for a show?" I jokingly called out over the spray of the water.

She said nothing, just sat back on the bench leaning into the vanity with a curious expression on her face. I quickly washed and rinsed my body and completed the rest of my morning ritual. Through it all, Bee followed as if some sort of invisible thread linked us, but still said nothing. After a quick call to the front desk to line up a car, I grabbed a light jacket—headed toward the door. Bee remained silent as we descended into the hotel lobby, waiting for the car to take us to the first destination. She wasn't pouting or obstinate, just eerily silent. It was kind of creeping me out, but I knew once we reached the place she wouldn't be able to shut up.

Ever since we'd seen the movie *Around the World in Eighty Days* as kids, Bee had been obsessed with riding in a hot air balloon. As far as I knew, she hadn't been up in one yet, so I arranged a sunrise balloon ride. The hot air balloon ride was set to take an hour, floating us about four thousand feet above ground through the Las Vegas sky. We would see views of The Strip, Las Vegas City and Red Rock Canyon while sailing at a smooth eight miles per hour. We pulled into the field to see the workers unfurling the balloon, its bold colors vibrant against the reddish brown rocks of the desert.

"Is that...are we...shut up. SHUT. UP!" Bee shrieked, hitting my bicep with each word.

Our car had barely come to a complete stop before she had the door open, running across the field to get closer to the action. I gave the driver pick up instructions and then slowly walked over to join her. Bee was paying me no attention at all, as she was completely enthralled by the process of the balloon's inflation and our eventual ascent. While Bee was otherwise entertained, I checked in with a harried looking young woman who buzzed about with a clipboard ensuring all passengers had paid and signed waivers. I walked over to Bee who was standing about ten feet from the nearly fully inflated balloon, eyes wide with her hands covering her mouth. She rocked on the balls of her feet, joy beaming from every bounce. I could tell it was taking everything within her not to squeal aloud. I stood behind her, my hands at her waist, pulling her close to place a kiss to her temple.

"Good surprise?"

"Great surprise."

An older white guy who looked like the textbook replica of Santa Claus called for the group to come closer together so he could give us the rules of flying. His name was Captain Bill and he was going to be responsible for navigating our flight today. After ensuring we understood the rules and risks associated with going up in the balloon, they allowed us to climb into the wicker basket. I was certain that we'd be pretty cramped with little room to maneuver, but the area we were in was actually quite spacious. Bee had made sure we were in close range to Captain Bill and hadn't stopped peppering him with questions since we'd boarded. After a while, I hustled Bee away from Captain Bill so we could enjoy the ride together. I completely understood her excitement, but had underestimated the depth of her obsession. She could have easily kept talking to Bill about balloons for the entirety of our ride.

"Hi, remember me?" I said, grabbing her arm to bring her back where I was standing.

She blushed slightly before responding, "Hey."

"So does this put me in the boyfriend hall of fame or nah?"

"How did you even know I've always wanted to go up in one of these?"

"Do you not remember that we were at *my* house when your obsession started?"

I'd been tasked with babysitting, as our mothers wanted a night out. Everett and Cadence had knocked out on us pretty quickly, but Bee hung in there. We were flipping through the channels trying to find something to watch when we happened on *Around the World in Eighty Days*. I thought it looked like a shitty movie, but Bee was insistent on watching it. I barely remembered what the movie was about, but I do remember Bee's awe about watching the characters travel from one destination to another in the hot air balloon.

"Oh my god, that's right. When you let me watch that terrible movie because I whined until you gave me the remote. One of my finer moments, obviously..."

Captain Bill clapped to get everyone's attention to let us know we would be landing soon. As we got into position for landing, Bee reached over, grabbing my forearm.

"El?"

"Yes?"

"Did I thank you?"

"For?"

"This," she said, gesturing around, "I can't believe you remembered this after all these years have passed. I just...it means more to me that I could ever say. Thank you so much!"

"Anything to see you smile."

The balloon company had champagne and orange juice waiting for us for post-flight mimosas, so we indulged in that while we waited for the car to come pick us up to take us to our next destination. Bee kept Captain Bill hemmed up with more questions about flying his balloon and I was so thankful when the car service finally appeared. We hopped into the car to get to our next destination, The Stratosphere Hotel.

I'd recently learned that Bee wanted to go skydiving, but that ain't quite a thing I wanted fuck with, so I found the next best thing—The Sky Jump at the Stratosphere. It was an eight hundred foot harnessed free fall, which came complete with a wrist cam to capture your descent. I wasn't too cool on willingly jumping off a building, but I also could not let my girl punk me, so I booked us both a jump. In hindsight it wasn't as bad as I anticipated it would be, but Bee would not stop teasing me about screaming like a little bitch the entire way down. It also didn't help that she had the workers send the video captured from the wrist cam directly to her email, which was accessible via her phone. So on the ride back to the Drake, she played that damn video at least five times, laughing hysterically.

———

"Bruh, I thought this was supposed to be a celebration. Sending our boy out in style. This shit is wack, man," my friend Trevor said, as we started a new game of Texas Hold 'Em.

He was right. The novelty of exclusivity wore off and now we were a group of five dudes, sitting miserably in a private gambling room, halfheartedly playing cards. Even the dealer had grown bored of us, mainly because we were such a sorry bunch that could barely get a good grasp on the rules of the game. Gambling had never been my thing and there was only so much cognac and cigars that I could take. I'd been with these knuckleheads for the better part of a few hours and I was pretty much over it and ready to call it a night.

"How are we in Vegas and I haven't seen one bare ass?" Mike yelled from across the room, "Where are the strippers?"

"Damn man, we can't have a classy night out for once? Why we gotta be worried about seeing some ass shake? I'm getting married tomorrow man. I'm off that," Trey said.

"Demi said no, huh?" Trevor asked.

"She didn't *outright* say it, but did express her opinion about exploitation of women at the hands of men at bachelor parties on a few different occasions. After laying that guilt trip on me, she then said to do what I wanted to do or whateva..."

"So we had to do this boring shit instead? Man, you might as well just signed us up for a wine and painting class, bruh. Same level of bull," Mike groused.

"Did you tell D she couldn't have strippers either?" Trevor piped up, holding up his phone. "Because Tami just tweeted a picture of the girls out and I definitely see a girl on a pole in the background over there."

"Ain't that a bitch? You can't exploit women, but she can watch stranger wangs flapping about in the breeze," muttered Mike.

"Nigga, did you just say stranger wangs? He said a girl on the pole," I laughed, damn near choking on my drink.

"You heard what I said."

Mike did have a point, though. Not that I cared one way or the other, but it was mad hypocritical for the girls to get to see a show while all we got to see was each other losing our hard-earned money to the house.

"Let me see that pic," Mike said, reaching for Trev's phone. "I know every strip club in this area like the back of my hand. We are crashing their shit."

And that's how we ended up turning separate bachelor and bachelorette parties into a coed free for all. I sat on the edge of the group, on a barstool peeping the scene. Mike looked as happy as a pig in shit since we'd ended up at a club full of women who didn't know how weak his game was. I looked over to see Demi sitting in Trey's lap, swaying back and forth to the music. The look on Trey's face was one of sheer pleasure as he wrapped his arms around her tighter, whispering something into her ear that made her blush. Shortly thereafter, the two of them bid us all a good night and skated out of the club quickly.

I sat sipping my drink, watching Bee talked animatedly with her hands to Cara, Demi's Maid of Honor. Whatever she was talking about had to be amusing because Cara was barely able to maintain her composure as she doubled over laughing. I finished my drink and walked over to the couch where Bee and Cara were sitting. Seeing my approach, Cara wrapped up her convo with Bee as I was sitting down.

"Hey."

"Hiiiiiiii," Bee slurred as she moved closer to me.

I lowered my head for a quick kiss and could taste the bourbon on her tongue.

"It's a good night?"

"I'm drunk."

"So you've had a good time then?"

"The best time. Demi is so nice. And her friends. All perf. Everything is awesome."

"You ready to call it a night?"

"You tryna put me to bed?"

"Tomorrow's gonna be a long day...and if you keep drinking, a rough one. Just looking out for your best interests."

Devorah didn't respond, just looked at me with a small smile playing on her features. Still not saying a word, she stood, swaying slightly in her heels. I stood quickly to steady her, placing an arm around her waist.

As she leaned into me she said, "You know what?"

"...no, what?"

"You're so good to me. And good for me. And I think I luh...I think I like *like* you."

Amused, I replied, "Well I know I like *like* you, too."

I expected Bee to be hungover the next morning, but she was awake and ready to go *way* earlier that I was. When I finally woke up, it was to a note saying that Demi had invited her over to the suite at the Venetian to get dressed with the rest of the ladies. We were the only ones in the group not staying at the Venetian — where the ceremony, dinner, and post-nuptial turn up were taking place — so I probably should have booked us there. But I was more concerned with showing off for my girl. Besides, it wasn't shit to me getting ready for the wedding outside of putting on the tux, lining up my beard and making sure my boutonniere was straight, so I spent the morning taking advantage of the private lap pool that was only available to those in the penthouse suites at the Drake.

I was tripping slightly because I wanted to talk to Bee about her l-word almost slip last night. At the risk of sounding carried away with feelings associated with this wedding, I felt like we were definitely in a place where we shouldn't have to be liquored up to express our true feelings about each other. Despite having not said it verbally, she had to know that I was unequivocally in love with her by now, right? Last night wasn't the best opportunity because I wanted her to hear those words from me when she was cognizant and clearly able to say them back to me. Otherwise, what the hell was the point? I knew one thing was for sure; we weren't getting on a plane back home before having a serious conversation about what we were doing, how we felt about each other, and finally coming out to our damn parents. I picked up my phone to send Bee a text and saw I had a missed call and text from Trey.

Worst Best Man Ever. Where the hell you at? — Trey Ball

Calm down, nigga. I'm on my way to
hold your hanky.

Oh you got jokes. I'll remember this
shit when it's your turn. — Trey Ball

The ceremony went off without a hitch, though it was
a bit weird to be a witness to a wedding that was essen-
tially happening in the middle of a shopping mall. Apparently Demi was *catching a vibe*, whatever the hell that
meant, from the Bridge of Love so they decided upon that
spot being the place to get married. The inside of the
Venetian was like a replica of the streets of Venice, replete
with canals and gondolas maneuvering through. The
bridge on which the wedding was held was a very small,
roped off intimate area with a few seats for everyone
besides the happy couple, Cara, the officiant, and me. Bee
sat in the front row, dabbing her tears as Trey and Demi
pledged their undying love to one another. I had to admit
I got a little choked up when Demi first appeared. Seeing
Trey completely break down upon seeing his bride for the
first time had all of our eyes tight.

After the ceremony, we headed over to TAO for
dinner. How we went from catching a Venetian vibe to
Asian vibe, I wasn't quite sure, but I was rollin' with it.
During dinner Bee was unusually quiet again. I asked if
everything was okay and she assured me it was. The only
time I got her to perk up was when I asked if she wanted
to take one of those gondola rides after we finished up
with dinner. She enthusiastically agreed and we split from
the group. We'd catch up with them at TAO the nightclub
after taking a slight detour to the gondolas. The newly
minted bride and groom reserved tables for us to pop
bottles in celebration of their love for the duration of the
night.

As we stood in line awaiting our gondola ride, I grabbed Bee's hand turning her to face me.

"So last night..." I started.

"I know," she cut me off, "I got a little drunk. Okay a lot drunk. Oh my god I wasn't annoying, was I? Cade always says there's a fine line between being adorably drunk and annoyingly drunk. Did I cross the line? Did someone say something to you?"

"Hey. Calm down. Nothing like that. I just wanted to ask if you remember what you said to me. When we were getting ready to leave...?"

"I...um...what?"

Devorah pulled away from me slightly, tucking her head. I immediately grasped her hand again, drawing her flush against me. The line inched up slightly; so I pushed her ahead, still keeping our fingers linked and her attention on me.

"Oh no you don't. Do you or do you not remember?"

"Remember telling you that I like you? Of course I remember that."

"You hesitated. You said you luh...like me. Not a stutter. A hesitation, a truncating of words or thoughts."

"I said what I said."

"So that's it? Oh wait...you don't wanna say it first. Well, well, well, wait 'til I tell CadyMac she was right."

"I don't know what you're..." she trailed off, eyes glazing over as she stiffened in my embrace.

She made a move to step out of my arms, but I held tightly to her waist with my left hand, while using the right to regain eye contact.

"I want you to be looking at me when I say this so you know it's real. I love you, Devorah Nicole Lee."

"Scoot? Devvy? I thought that was you all!" I heard a familiar voice say.

"Mama?"

I turned around to see my parents standing about fifteen feet behind us in line. *What in the hell were they doing in Vegas?* Bee quickly pulled out of my embrace, looking like her worst nightmare had come true. My mother talked her way closer to us, asking folks if they'd mind her and my father moving ahead of them in line so that they would not have to shout past them to talk to us. By the time my parents had reached us, Bee looked like she wanted to be anywhere but in this line.

"See EJ, I told you that was my boy. I'd recognize that head anywhere," my mother said, pulling me into a quick hug before moving over to hug and speak with Bee. I couldn't hear their conversation, but from the look on Devorah's face I knew it was anything but good.

"What are y'all doing in Vegas, Pops? You didn't mention anything about going out of town last time I saw you."

"This was your mother's doing. Some last minute thing she put together talking 'bout she wanted to see Celine Dion before her residency ended. We got here and found out the damn show was going to be around 'til 2019. Your mother must have heard wrong on the program she was watching."

He looked none too pleased about being in Vegas or seeing Celine Dion. I knew my father well enough to know that whatever Miranda Taylor wanted, Miranda Taylor got. So though he grumbled and seemed agitated with being here, I knew he was secretly pleased that he was able to keep his lady smiling.

"Scooter...I told Devvy we should see if you all's private

gondola can fit two more. We were gonna be riding with strangers, but isn't this great that we're all here together now?"

Turned out that the private gondolas were the same size as the regular gondolas, so all four of us piled in to set off on the short ride. My parents sat on the side of the boat near the gondolier and I tried to usher Bee to the other set of seats, but she jerked away as soon as I touched her arm. She'd been quiet as we waited, but the tension emanating from her was palpable. My mother had hemmed the gondolier up with small talk before we pushed off, so I turned to Bee.

"Hey," I said, nudging her arm to get her to look at me.

"Don't fucking hey me. How could you?" she whispered.

"How could I what? What are you talking about?"

"Oh so they just happened to be here? And taking a gondola ride at the same time as us? I'm supposed to believe this is all coincidence? I can't believe you would do this to me."

Wait...what? She could not have possibly thought that I set this all up. Why in the hell would I? I told her I would give her time to be comfortable with rolling our relationship out to the family on her terms. What would I stand to gain by forcing her into it? Nothing but the grief I was currently getting.

"What are you two lovebirds over there whispering about?" my mother asked, grinning widely.

"Sir?" Bee snapped, seeking the attention of the gondolier, "Can we go ahead and get this over with?"

A bit taken aback, the gondolier shoved off the dock and began paddling while singing in slightly broken Italian. Bee sat with her arms folded, body angled away from the rest of us, staring out into the faux Venetian canals. My mother tried to engage her a couple times, but her answers were terse and super short. When the ride came to an end, she barely waited for the gondolier's okay to disembark from the boat before she climbed over me, taking off. She ran through the casino at a clip and I tried in vain to catch her. Guess I should have been working harder on cardio instead of weights in the gym because she dusted me. By the time I'd reached the main entrance, she was in a cab, presumably headed back to our hotel. I shot Trey a quick text letting him know we wouldn't be making it to the after party and got in a cab to the Drake.

I walked into a dark, empty suite. I flipped on the lights and saw that everything was exactly as it had been when I left, so Bee hadn't been here at all. There were at least ten minutes between her cab taking off and me actually being able to get one, so there was no way I could have beat her back. I called, but she didn't answer. Sent her a text immediately after for her to let me know she was okay. I took an elevator down to the casino level to see if she was down there in the bar area, but she was nowhere to be found. I even asked a few of the workers if they had seen her and no one had. Half an hour passed and I still hadn't heard from her. By this time I was crazy with worry because she hadn't responded to any of my texts and was, by all accounts, missing. I knew she wasn't upset enough to just go straight to the airport without luggage or anything, so she would have to come back to the room eventually—unless she was hurt or injured in some way. I tried to put the thought of her being in harm's way out of my mind and decided to wait it out before I got the local authorities involved.

While I waited, my mother called to make sure everything was okay with Bee. She wanted to go to the police immediately, but my father talked her down. I filled her in on what I'd walked back into and my game plan. She also admitted that the reason that they were in Vegas wasn't just to see Celine. Apparently she had her suspicions that I was seeing someone and would be bringing whoever it was to Vegas with me for the wedding. She and those friends of hers cooked up this harebrained scheme to come out here and accidentally bump into me in the hotel. She knew the wedding was at the Venetian thanks to creeping on Trey's Facebook, but had no idea I wasn't actually staying there. Convincing my dad to take her on the gondola ride was coincidental, but fortuitous on her end. She had been shocked when she realized my mystery lady was Devorah.

Another half an hour had passed when I finally heard the door to the suite open. I rushed toward the front of the suite, pulling Devorah into a hug, relieved that was she was safe and sound. I asked where she had been, but there was no response. She angrily pushed out of my embrace, stepping around me, as she walked toward the bedroom area of the suite.

"Really, Bee? Silent treatment? Real mature..."

She shot me a look meant to pierce my soul as she moved around the gathering her belongings and stuffing them in her bag.

"So you're really not going to talk to me?"

"What do you want me to say?"

"You could start with telling me why you ran off like a crazy woman and had me worried sick about your goddamn whereabouts for the past ninety minutes. That would be perfect, in fact."

"How about you start with why the hell you set me up? Let's start there. Did you Google 'how to force your girlfriend into revealing your relationship to disapproving parents'? Is that where this ridiculous idea of having your mom and dad pop up on us came from?"

"You can't be serious. Why in the hell would I have orchestrated this? What could I stand to gain?"

"I have no idea what you had in mind. Just like your brother, two slithering, sneaky snakes ass dudes. You probably were the main one telling him to fuck around on Cass. Lulling me into a false sense of security."

"You realize you're making no sense, right? Why are you talking about Cass and Ev? What do they have to do with you being mad that you erroneously thought I intentionally asked my parents to show up in Vegas? This is silly. You're being dramatic."

"This isn't silly nor am I being dramatic. What part of...wait, why am I even still talking to you?"

She resumed throwing things in her bag, scrambling to ensure she left nothing behind.

"Devorah...let's just take a time out."

"Fuck a time out. I'm just out period."

"Where are you going?"

"Don't worry about where I'm going."

"You need to calm down before you leave to go anywhere."

Devorah kept walking toward the front door of the suite. Before striding out of the door, she turned back to me and said, "Do me a favor. Erase my existence from your consciousness."

11

DEVORAH

Six weeks later...

"Well aren't you a sorry sight."

"Immy!"

Those words floated over my shoulder from the last voices I wanted to hear. I'd been doing a really good job at avoiding one of them for the past few weeks, feigning work deadlines and fatigue every time she called. The other I hadn't seen since that fateful night in Vegas and was sure she had an earful for me. They, along with my Aunt Berta barged into my living room with Cadence trailing behind them, looking contrite.

"I was gonna ask how y'all got in here, but..."

"Sorry, sis. I was ambushed."

"So naturally you set me up for the same?"

I was actually surprised that it took them this long to come ream me out. My mama and her friends were an opinionated bunch and I just knew that after Auntie Randi rolled up on Ellis and I in Vegas that I would be hearing from Imogene Landon-Lee immediately. But beyond her normal wellness checks, my mama hadn't said a word to me about whatever Ellis and me...*were*. We hadn't spoken since Vegas, despite his initial attempts to talk some sense into me. I had it in my brain that I had been bamboozled, hoodwinked and led astray, so his words fell on deaf ears. A few weeks of space, perspective, and clarity soon had me realizing that I'd fucked up royally. My pride, however, wouldn't allow me to admit that mistake to him. Instead I replayed that night in my head over and over, berating the choices I made that led to this fucked up mess of a lonely life I was now committed to.

While we were standing in line for the gondolas, I saw the profile of an older couple that looked vaguely familiar join the line about fifteen folks behind us. The man in the couple turned his head and my worst fears were confirmed, it was Auntie Randi and Uncle EJ. Uncle EJ and I made eye contact immediately and I saw him try to deflect Auntie Randi's attention, talking her out of the gondola ride. I couldn't hear what they were saying, but his words were clearly not being absorbed as Auntie Randi stood her ground in the line. As the line shifted, I tried to put some space between us, but Ellis was insistent on keeping his hands on me. I swear I must have blacked out because the only thing I remembered after that was Auntie Randi and Uncle EJ popping up right behind us in line. Ellis' declaration of love barely registered as his mom and dad appeared over his shoulder, catching us in a definitely more than friendly embrace.

After that was the world's most awkward gondola ride with me, El, Aunt Randi and Uncle EJ. The ride was maybe ten minutes total, but it felt like ten years. Not many words were exchanged and as soon as we got back to the dock, I hopped out of that gondola and took off. Ellis tried in vain to chase behind me, but I ran like the hounds of hell were chasing me. I had no particular destination in mind; I just knew I needed to get the hell out of there. I ended up sitting in front of the fountain at the Bellagio for an embarrassingly long amount of time staring at the water and wondering how I could have missed what appeared to be an obvious set up. It could not have just been coincidence that the one weekend we were in Vegas, Ellis' parents just happened to be there as well. And also happened to be going on a gondola ride when we were. I felt incredibly betrayed and set up when he knew my feelings about revealing our relationship to our parents.

When I finally made it back to our suite at the Drake, Ellis looked completely ashen. His relief at me finally making my way back quickly turned to anger as we argued about his parents magically appearing. I called him everything but a child of God as I went on and on about him being a snake in the grass lowlife just like his little brother. After telling him to erase my existence from his consciousness, I haphazardly packed my bag and went straight to the airport, trying to get as far away from that disaster as quickly as possible.

It took coming home and talking it through with Celena and Cadence to allow me to see what a colossal mistake I'd made. I was so quick to think the worst of Ellis that I hadn't considered the possibility of anything, but him bullying me into doing this relationship on his terms. I'd placed all of his previous concessions aside, wholly convinced that he was placing his wants and needs above my own, at my expense. I'd spent the weeks since Vegas throwing myself into work; weeknights and weekends spend lazing around on my couch watching HGTV and SVU alternately. In the beginning Ellis contacted me frequently trying to get me to see his side, but I was just too embarrassed by the way I'd handled myself to even talk to him. Cade told me I needed to get over myself and follow my bliss, but by the time I'd decided to do just that, El was no longer picking up the phone.

So this delayed ambush or intervention by my mama

and her friends was just odd to me, honestly. I had no idea what to even expect with them showing up.

"So you done feeling sorry for yourself or what?" my mother asked.

"Imogene, must you be so..."Auntie Randi started.

"Must you be an asshole? That is really what she wanted to know, Imogene?" Auntie Berta interrupted.

"Well not in those exact words, but yes...that."

"Oh please, Devorah is a grown woman. She should be able to handle anything I've got to say. I mean by this point she has to know she was a damn fool."

A fool? Color me shocked, but that was certainly the last thing I'd ever expected to hear coming out of my mother's mouth. Jezebel, harlot, skank, or brotherfucker all would have been more expected than fool.

"So are y'all gonna keep talking about me like I'm not here or...?"

"Depends on whether or not you're gonna get yourself together and tell me why you've broken my baby's heart and how you're gonna fix your screw up."

My eyebrows rose damn near to my hairline. I expected the sass from my mother, but not from Auntie Randi. She was the most even keeled of the three. Mama was the asshole. Auntie Berta was the straight shooter. All four women in the room stared at me with expectant looks on their faces. My shock gave way to confusion as I realized that the wrath I thought I'd face from them regarding starting a relationship with Ellis was nowhere to be found.

"Well?" my mom prompted.

"Time out. Y'all are mad at me for...what exactly?"

"I have no idea of why the other ladies are upset with you, but as for me? Three reasons — the first being that you didn't feel like you could trust me enough to tell me that it was Ellis you were dating when I specifically asked you about your love life. I understand your hesitance because of the mess that happened with that other young man, but I thought that was water under the bridge. Secondly, I'm mad that you broke that boy's heart. I was at Randi's for Sunday dinner last week and he looked like someone had stolen his bike or kicked his puppy. You know I look at those boys like my own sons and to know he was in pain because of *my* child just about killed me. And lastly...I didn't raise no punk. So I know good and well you have realized your mistakes and want to get back with that boy, but are over here cowering in fear because you think it's too late. I'm pissed that you're a coward and I'm hurt that you didn't trust me enough to bring this to me, but instead chose to dodge my calls and act like your lil raggedy life really had something going on."

My mother stopped her rant to take a breath and Auntie Randi took over. Her voice was devoid of the previous irritation when she addressed me again. My guess would be the tears that I was unable to tamp down during my mother's rant were the reason that she switched over to her normal, gentle tone when she asked me one question.

"So what are you going to do?"

I took a couple minutes to get myself together, trying to control my breathing enough to speak without bursting into sobs. Cadence moved from her spot on my chaise, to wrap an arm around my shoulder, patting it in a comforting manner. I was finally able to calm down a little bit before I spoke.

"I...I don't know. I really messed this all up."

"Baby, why did you think you had to lie to everybody?" my mother asked, her tone more conciliatory than before.

I shrugged, "I thought you wouldn't approve."

Because that is what everything boiled down to, honestly. I was so concerned with how things would appear to them, not even taking into consideration that they would place our happiness above all else. I had already had it in my mind that I would be condemned for dallying with both of Auntie Randi's sons. Never mind the fact that Everett and I hadn't been with each other in over ten years nor that what Ellis and I shared was the closest thing to *the real thing* than I'd ever felt in my life. It was all about how I thought I would be perceived. I never once took into consideration how all of this affected him. He was so affable, rolling with the punches and accepting my ridiculous ass rules that I didn't even think about the fact that he too was charged with lying to his parents and keeping up a charade for no reason. Sitting here being lectured about breaking his heart just made me feel worse, honestly.

"Why wouldn't we approve, Devvy? Y'all are two adults in a consenting relationship. And from what I could tell by observing you all for a little while before we approached, a loving and stable relationship. So what would there be to disapprove of?" Aunt Randi asked curiosity etched across her features.

I had no answer for her. I could run through my fears of them finding out, but that all seemed silly now in light of their reactions. All of this drama and strife was completely avoidable and unnecessary if I had just put on my big girl panties and let myself have this man, damn what anyone else had to say. All of my fears about our parents' reactions were unfounded.

"Nothing?" I responded.

"You don't sound too sure," Auntie Berta piped up.

She'd been conspicuously quiet through this entire intervention. Something that I was sure was a byproduct of Cade's interference.

"So again, I ask you, what are you going to do to right this? I'm tired of seeing my Scoot coming to my house looked all harried and bedraggled because he's throwing himself into work to numb his pain."

"I mean…I'm sure he doesn't want to talk to me."

"You'll never know unless you give it a try. You may very well be surprised," my mother said.

The other ladies all nodded their heads in agreement.

———

I spent the morning freaking out about what to wear. It was just another of SophieBean's recitals, so it wasn't like I had to be too fancy, but it would be the first time I'd seen Ellis since Vegas. I wanted to be looking *good*. No, better than good. I wanted to look *irresistible*. My hair, makeup and outfit were chosen to specifically appeal to the things Ellis loved most about me. Hair swept up in a topknot because he loved undoing it to run his fingers through my kinks and coils. Face mostly free of makeup beyond a swipe of gloss on my lips because he liked the way it made my lips look extra kissable. I settled on wearing one of my favorite wrap dresses, brightly patterned in magenta, grey and white paired with a low heeled magenta strappy sandal because he loved seeing my legs in dresses and appreciated the easy accessibility a wrap dress allowed.

My nervous energy led to me arriving at En Pointe way earlier than anticipated. The doors weren't open to the general public, so I went to a nearby coffee shop, Perk, to have a latte and calm my nerves. I hadn't really rehearsed what I would say to Ellis because I didn't want this to sound like a speech. I wanted to speak from the heart so he could really understand where I was coming from and — *hopefully* — find it in his heart to forgive me so that we could move past this drama. As I sat sipping my latte, staring out the window, and damn near ready to take my ass home, my phone buzzed.

Good luck girlie. Don't punk out. — **Yung Celly**

Girl. You know I was on my way.

I know. But you got this. Get your man back. — **Yung Celly**

What if it's too late?

It's never too late for true love. :) — **Yung Celly**

Yes, I know how corny that sounded before you clown me. — **Yung Celly**

I chucked at her swift back to back texts because she knew I was absolutely going to clown her for peak corniness. I'd never been that type of girl, the one who easily accepted that everyone eventually got a happily ever after. I was too practical for all of that. Life, love and relationships never got a cute little made-for-TV ending. There was always a sheen of strain that covered relationships. The good ones were cobbled together by a tenuous thread that, with too much pressure, could easily break. I finished my latte, steeled myself to see Ellis, and walked back to En Pointe.

When I walked in, all of the usual suspects were there sitting together, minus Ellis. Cass has assured me that he was coming when I spoke with her earlier this week about everything that had been going on. I made my way over to them, greeting everyone and settled in next to Auntie

Randi. She or Cass had made it so the seats that were saved for our crew forced Ellis and I to have to sit next to one another. We obviously couldn't speak during the show, but I was hoping he'd be here beforehand so we could talk. A few minutes passed with me making small talk with Auntie Randi and Uncle EJ before the dance instructor Mrs. Hampton came out to quiet everyone down so the show could begin.

The disappointment of Ellis not being there must have been evident on my face because Auntie Randi grabbed my hand, giving it a reassuring squeeze. I tried shifting my focus and putting Ellis' absence out of my mind as the three and four year olds shuffled through a routine set to an old Britney Spears tune. Watching the girls fumble their way through, yet persevering to the end brought a smile to my face. Just as the next routine was set to start, I felt his presence approaching before I actually saw him. When he reached our row, he hesitated before sitting down, briefly scanning the area to see if there were any other open seats. The tiny shred of hopefulness I'd been holding onto until that moment completely dissipated. He couldn't even bear to sit next to me for a ninety minute recital and I was supposed to be winning my way back into his heart with my words? *Shit*. The rest of the show passed in a blur for me. I was barely present, too consumed with what in the hell I was going to say to Ellis after the show.

"So, you do know you have to actually approach him to say something, right?" Cassidy said to me as we all filed out of the recital room to wait for Beanie so we could all go to Easy Sundae.

At her words my gaze traveled over to where El stood talking to Everett and Uncle EJ. He looked handsome as ever, milk chocolate skin shimmering against the stark white of the polo shirt he'd combined with dark rinse jeans and casual shoes. Either Ev or Uncle EJ had said something hilarious because he burst into loud laughter, a sound I hadn't realized I'd missed so much until hearing it just now.

"I can't telepathically beg for forgiveness?"

"Mmmm...nah. You gotta go over there and grovel in person."

"I don't wanna interrupt."

"Bullshit, you're being a punk."

"What do I say, Cass?"

"Some variant of I fucked up, I'm sorry, how can I fix this? That's what Everett did."

"And that worked?"

We hadn't had a chance to really get together with me avoiding everyone to keep from having to talk about Ellis. When I arrived today, I noticed that Cass and Ev seemed to be their usual loving selves, but wasn't sure if it was a front or what.

"Not completely. But it was a start. We are still...and likely will forever be working through it. But this isn't about me right now. Stop stalling, take your behind over there, and start the process of getting your man back."

I took a deep breath, squared my shoulders and set off in the direction of the men. On my approach I greeted Ev and Uncle EJ with hugs and kisses. They quickly made themselves scarce as I turned to El. He looked as if he'd rather be anywhere but in this moment, speaking to me right now.

"Hey."

"Did you need something?"

"Can..." I trailed off, swallowing hard before trying again, "Can we talk?"

"About...?"

"Us?" I squeaked out.

Legs braced apart, hands resting by his side, Ellis replied, "I'm listening."

And I was stuck. Everything I'd thought about saying to him had completely left my mind. I felt foolish, standing there as he looked positively bored and disinterested in anything I had to say. This was dumb. He clearly had moved on and didn't give a damn about me or us anymore. Why should I even try?

Clearing my throat I said, "I just wanted to say..."

"Let's goooooo, guys!" a small voice interrupted. Sophie snuck between the two of us, grabbing our hands, urging us toward the door.

"Sophia Lauren Taylor, get your behind over here now!"

"But mama, I just wanted..."

"You just wanted your tail embarrassed in front of all your little friends is what you just wanted. Don't make me tell you to get over here again."

Sophie's shoulders slumped as she walked back to where everyone else was standing.

"You were saying?" Ellis prompted.

Still a little dumbfounded I replied, "I...we should probably get going to Easy Sundae before the Bean gets too restless."

Ellis' mouth opened like he was going to say something, but instead he nodded, turned on his heel and walked away.

"So you punked out?" Cadence said.

Instead of going to Easy Sundae with everyone for ice cream I headed home. On my drive, Cade called to see how things went. After running down the story to her, she and Celena were on my doorstep half an hour later with

Ciao Bella blood orange sorbet and a bottle of Petite Syrah.

"It...I...it just didn't seem like the right time."

Cadence and Celena shared a look before Cel spoke up.

"And what exactly would the right time look like, Dev?"

"I don't...know. Y'all didn't see how he looked at me. I....maybe too much time passed. I...he...I don't know, y'all. I think I was too late."

"Dev, with all due respect? That is the biggest load of bullshit I've ever heard. I haven't known you as long as Cade, but I'm sure she'll agree with me when I say that you were at your absolute best when you guys were together. I'd never seen you more free despite the weight of your silly ass 'don't tell my mama' complex you had going on. And if you love that man as much as you say you love him, then any time is the right time. Stop being a punk. Go get your man back. For real this time."

I looked at Cadence to see if she had anything to add, but she remained quiet. I knew she had an inkling of what Ellis truly felt, but I'd avoided asking her anything about him directly. Mainly because I couldn't bear facing the reality that I'd really fucked up and lost him for good. I took her encouraging me to go after him as an early sign that there was still a chance, but her silence now had me worried.

"Oh, you want me to be the oracle. You want me to give you hope because you know El and I are close and we've talked about this? Sorry, sis. Not this time. You fucked up. I mean, *royally*. And I'm low-key mad at you because I spent all of my time telling El to be gentle with your heart and what do you do? You Gallaghered the shit outta his."

"Gallaghered?"

"You know that crazy ass white man, with the fucked up hair who be smashing watermelons and shit with sledgehammers? Gallagher. Anyway, I've been being easy because I saw your pain, but I'm tired of handling you with kid gloves. Put on your big girl panties. Do the grand gesture! Own your shit. Grovel. Plead. Beg. And hopefully get your man back. And if not? Then reflect on this as a lesson of shit to never, ever, *ever* do again in life."

———

I felt like an idiot. I was standing on Ellis' stoop with an arm full of poster boards, a tote bag of various other props slung over my arm, and the last shred of hope to which I clung tightly. After Cade read me the riot act, one thing stood out; her telling me to do the grand gesture. What better way to win back the man whose favorite movie genre — that he'd never admit in mixed company — was the romantic comedy. In all of the movies we'd watched there became a point where the guy in the relationship fucked up. And every single time, they did some out of the box thing to get the girl back. So I was doing the thing. Or at least attempting to do the thing and hoping to get the guy back. I rang the doorbell and waited nervously. This thing could either go really well or tank incredibly fast.

12

ELLIS

When I answered my doorbell, the last thing I expected to see was Bee standing there with her arms filled with a ton of crap and a tote bag over her shoulder, looking scared shitless. I wasn't surprised to see her standing on the other side of the door as CadyMac had alluded to her coming to pay her penance in person, but the props threw me for a loop. She tried approaching me at Sophie's recital and I'd admit to being a bit of an asshole then. I was still hurting... hell, *am still hurting* if we're being honest and I didn't want a hollow ass apology. I wanted her to be real with me and let me in. Explain exactly what the hell was going on her in her head, no matter how crazy or how much she didn't think I would understand her train of thought. I deserved at least that much. We wouldn't have even had to go through all of this ridiculous shit if she had kept it a buck at the beginning.

After Vegas I kept calling, texting...hell I even popped up at her job unexpectedly a few times and nothing. So I stopped. I loved her. *Love* her. But I was not chasing anyone who didn't want to be chased. Trey said this was my comeuppance for all the stunts I'd pulled over the years. I'd never wanted to punch anyone more than in the moment he said that. It was the truth though, kind of. All of my manwhoring and Black Clooney antics culminated me in being brought to my knees by a woman who didn't want to give me the time of day. Who woulda thought? I stood in the doorway, arms crossed, one eyebrow cocked.

"Um...hey."

"You need something?"

"I...," Bee started before clearing her throat and beginning again. "Yeah, I need you to just shut up and just read. Okay?"

Shock stretched across my features as I nodded slowly. I had no idea where she was going with this, but...okay. I leaned against the doorframe, gesturing for her to go ahead and do whatever it was she was going to do. My relaxed stance seemed to shift her energy from nervous to anticipatory. She sat the poster boards facedown while messing around with her phone to connect it to the Bluetooth speaker she took out of the tote bag. Some song started playing with a thumping bass beat and some chick with an oddly weird yet, pleasant voice starting singing about...something I could barely make out because Bee held up the first of the poster boards for me to read. It said:

I KNOW I FUCKED UP, RIGHT?

I couldn't help but laugh because I certainly did not expect that.

"Don't answer. I already know I did. My mama, your mama, Cadence, Celena, Cassidy...hell even cheater cheater pumpkin eater Everett gave me an earful. And I had to sit with it for some time. Because I was so sure I was right. I was super certain that you'd forced my hand because you were getting tired of me and knew I'd go off the handle if my hand was forced, right?"

I opened my mouth to speak, but she raised a hand to stop me.

"I...I gotta get this out. Just keep reading. And listening. There will be a review and Q&A session at the end."

She held up the next two boards.

SO WHAT HAPPENS WHEN THEY FUCK UP IN THE MOVIES?
THEY DO THE GRAND GESTURE.

"So this is mine. I'm ol dude with the boombox in Say Anything. Homie with the cue cards in Love Actually. Taye Diggs at the radio station in Brown Sugar. Giving my last ditch effort to let you know that I've seen the error of my ways. And I'm sorry. Really and truly sorry and I want you to know two things..."

First board she held up said...

I'M JUST A GIRL. STANDING IN FRONT OF A BOY. ASKING
HIM TO LOVE HER.

"And also..."

I LOVE YOU. AND THAT'S URGENT LIKE A MOTHERFUCKER.

"In case you hadn't seen Notting Hill, I had to double down with one of the worst films committed to cellulose triacetate, Love Jones."

"What in the hell is cellu..."

"Hey! I'm not done. Q&A at the end!"

She pulled out her phone, switching from the low r&b music that had been playing during her soliloquy to one that was decidedly more pop rockish. She let the guitar intro play for a couple seconds before she fast forwarded to what I assumed was the chorus which she let play before turning the music back down. Some angsty white girl singing about how her life would suck without some dude, presumably. I laughed again, which I could tell bolstered her courage a bit as she continued.

"So as Kelly just sang, my life would suck without you permanently. Having a taste of it these past few weeks almost took me out the game. So here I am. Laying it all on the line, saying it plain. I love you, Ellis. I'm so deeply, foolishly, unequivocally in love with you that it makes me scared to admit, but I'd rather be with you than without. After our mamas got in my behind about my behavior, I replayed that night in Vegas in my mind over and over again. You put your feelings out there and I completely ignored them because of my own insecurities. I'm not promising you that I'm completely healed, but I'm here today to show you that I'm ready to do the work. I'm stepping out on faith that if you really loved me like you said you did, you'd forgive me. And we'd start over. So..."

She reached into her tote bag, handing me a comically large marker and held up one last poster board.

WILL YOU BE MY BOYFRIEND AGAIN?
[ ] YES [ ] NO [ ] MAYBE

She looked so adorable, face full of hope as she shyly smiled and gestured for me to make my choice.

"Can I have some time to think about it?" I asked.

Her face fell instantly before she quickly schooled her

features into a mask of nonchalance. She turned and started gathering the poster boards and her speaker.

"Yeah...that's...um...sure. Just, uh...you know the number. I'm gonna just, um...I'll talk to you later?"

She started down the stairs, then turned around to hand me the last poster board.

"I'll let you hold onto this one."

"Bee?"

"Yeah?"

"I love you."

Her eyes widened, before a small smile emerged on her face.

"I love you, too."

"I'll talk to you later, okay?"

"Ah...okay."

Her descent of the stairs was a bit less weighed down this time. I watched her walk down to her car, get in and take off before going back inside. Once inside, I went looking for my phone to make a quick phone call.

"I need your help."

———

"You know this is some crazy shit, right?"

"She out romanced me, yo. I couldn't let her win."

Cadence laughed as she crossed the threshold.

"Oh my God, it smells amazing in here."

"Told you I'd deliver."

"Yeah yeah yeah."

I wasn't a *complete* asshole. See...before Bee came over with her cute ass poster board declarations and speech and shit, I'd been plotting. In the time we'd been apart, I'd been thinking...*just like her*. And I'd made up my mind that

I was done with the silly shit...*just like her*. But I'd also wanted to make her sweat a little bit. I was waiting for CadyMac to give me the all clear before I enacted Operation Woo. I wasn't going down without a fight. Everything was out in the open and despite her less than stellar reaction to us being outed; I *knew* that she was it. At the wedding, watching Trey and Demi pledge their undying love for each other—it hit me. That's such a cliché right?

"You realize I've had to hold sister circle vigils with her and Celena for the past two days because 'I poured my fucking heart out and he didn't even caaaaaaare'. Why do y'all insist on keeping the pregnant lady in the midst of your drama?"

"I can't talk about this shit with Trey or any of my boys, CadyMac. *C'mon.* You know that. Ev ain't got time since he's doing overtime trying to get his wife back, so..."

"I get the logic, bro. Truly. I do. But, I thought you already fucking had the ring, dude. Why are you prolonging this?"

"Because you let her out romance me! I know that grand gesture shit was all you!"

"There is something truly wrong with you, you know that? *Please* tell me you're going to talk to that girl today."

"I am. You wanna see it?"

"Hell yes I want to see it. Why in the hell do you think I came by?"

"You came over here because I promised you gumbo once you got the correct ring size for me," I said, stirring the simmering pot on the stove.

"And I fucking delivered!"

"Language, CadyMac! All this cursing while my niece is in utero."

"Just show me the damn ring."

I grabbed the box from the counter and walked it over to Cadence. I was nervous watching her open it because I didn't seek her counsel at all. I just asked her to get me Bee's ring size and assured her I'd take care of the rest. I mean, after all, I'd known the woman for the entirety of her life. I knew what she liked, her tastes and style...shit like that. But...this was different. If I was giving her what was supposed to be a token of my undying love for her, it needed to be a showstopper. I'd been researching gemstones for weeks because the one thing I knew for sure was she didn't want a diamond to be the centerpiece of the ring.

"Oh my God, El!"

"I did good?"

The ring was vintage inspired, with a cushion cut morganite as the centerpiece, set in a rose gold floral setting with a scalloped diamond band. The morganite stone was a beautiful pinkish peach sort of color, which complemented the rose gold of the band quite nicely. The moment I saw it, it screamed Devorah to me. I was relieved to get Cadence's stamp of approval.

"You did great. This is beautiful! So when are you...?"

"Tonight."

"Wait. You can't tonight."

"And why the hell not?"

"Her nails look a mess! You can't propose to the girl with her damn fingers looking crazy because she's been gnawing on them waiting for you to call."

"Cadence."

"Ellis."

"Seriously?"

"Yes! This is a thing. Trust me. Let me work this out. It has to be tonight, huh?"

"YES."

"Okay. Fine. Give me a few hours. I'll make sure her hands look presentable."

It had to be tonight because it had been exactly nine months since AdTech when we came to what was allegedly a no strings attached, no feelings caught understanding. Bee likely had no idea that from there we'd end up here, but I'd always known. All of my Black Clooney antics were my way of passing the time until we were really ready to do this. I knew I was really ready now and I hoped to God Bee was too.

I stood outside Bee's front door nervous as hell. I'd heard from Cadence hours ago that they did the nail thing and now it was show time. I shifted the poster board under my left arm and rang the doorbell. Instead of Devorah answering as expected, it was her friend Celena, who promptly shut the door in my face. *What the hell?* I rang the doorbell again, but it was a good two to three minutes before someone came back to the door again. It was Celena again, but this time she had a duffle slung over her arm. Passing me, she patted my shoulder saying, "She's in the front room. Good luck!"

I walked in and just as Celena said, there she was sitting on the love seat in her living room. I sat the poster board that was in my hands down in the chair to my right and sat down next to her, wrapping arm around her shoulders to bring her close to me. I pressed a quick kiss to her forehead and felt her relax in my arms instantly.

"Hey."

"Hi."

"How are you?"

"Stressed."

"What's going on?"

"I...can we skip the small talk? Can you just get on with what you're going to do?"

I pulled back a bit to look her in the eye and could see the sheen of unshed tears she tried valiantly to keep from falling.

"So about the question you asked the other day. I have an answer for you."

"Okay."

"Before I tell you though, I want you to let me finish completely before you respond, okay?"

Devorah nodded once. I grabbed the poster board where I sat it when I walked in. I'd checked the no box. I watched as she looked at the board dumbfounded.

"Turn it over."

On the opposite side of the board I'd written:

I'D RATHER BE YOUR HUSBAND.

Bee inhaled sharply as she processed what I'd written. While she was reading, I'd moved into position on one knee, grabbing her left hand.

"I know you're going to have a thousand reasons as to why we should wait, it's too soon blah blah blah, but I'm tired of playing. I love you and you claim to be deeply, madly, obsessively in love with..."

"Yes."

"Hold on woman, I'm not done! I had a whole speech. Let me...wait...yes?"

I looked up to see her nodding furiously, tears streaming. A huge sense of relief washed over me as I got up from the floor, pulling her into me for a real kiss. Before we got too carried away, however, I remembered we had somewhere to go. I pulled back, giving Bee one last soft kiss before telling her to put on some shoes. While she was getting herself together, I shot off a quick text to make sure everything was a go.

The first person I called that day I asked Bee for some time to think about her grand gesture was Aunt Imogene. I hadn't spoken to Uncle James in years, plus he and Devorah weren't super close so I didn't bother trying to track him down. I knew my dad still kept in touch with him, but for this I needed to engage the parent with which she had the most interaction. After a brief cryptic phone call, I went over to Auntie's house, laid out my intentions and asked for Devorah's hand. She granted it instantly, shockingly, citing that she always knew her baby would end up with one of Randi's boys.

We arrived at her mother's house and everyone was there waiting for us — my mother, father, Everett, Cassidy, Cadence, and Geoff. Hell even Uncle James was there, surprisingly. I knew that he and Aunt Im hadn't split on the best terms and despite it being over a decade, the wound was still a little raw. It was a major deal if she called him over to join us. Auntie Imogene went all out, a huge photo banner, with a picture of us I'd never seen before; congratulating us was draped across the mantle in her living room.

All of the women rushed Bee immediately asking to see the ring. *Shit!* I'd been so caught up in her actually saying yes, that I never even put the damn thing on her finger. I reached into my pocket as I walked over to where they were congregating and got down on one knee again as I placed the ring on her finger. The sharp intake of breath from Bee and collective *awwwww* from the rest of the ladies let me know I'd done a *great* job. They immediately peppered me with questions about the stone, where I'd gotten such a unique ring, and who had helped me pick it out. I think they were all very shocked that I didn't need any help finding the right ring.

Later that evening, Bee and I were relaxing at my place. We'd decided to crash there for the night since I lived closer to Auntie Im's and we were eager to celebrate our engagement the right way.

As we lay in bed Bee asked, "Why this stone? Why not a diamond?"

"Oh like I forgot the twenty minute lecture I got about diamonds after we watched that god awful DiCaprio film? Or how every time you saw an extravagantly large diamond you'd sigh in disgust. Oh please. I'm surprised you let me get away with the diamonds in the band, which...by the way, are conflict free."

"I love this morganite. It's such a beautiful, powerful stone."

"Powerful?"

"Yeah, you know mama is on her Google everything kick and she looked it up. Says it's supposed to provide relief and positivity during stressful times and aid in developing patience and communication skills."

"No wonder it screamed your name when I saw it!"

"Hey!"

"I mean..."

"Oh shut up. I got it right eventually, yes?"

"Took you long enough."

ABOUT THE AUTHOR

Nicole Falls is a contemporary Black romance writer who has taken entirely too long to complete her first project. She's also a ceramic mug and lapel pin enthusiast who cannot function without her wireless Beats constantly blaring music. When Nicole isn't writing, she spends her time trolling her friends and family while drinking coffee and/or cocktails or checking off yet another of these great United States visited in her quest to see some land! She currently resides in the suburbs of Chicago.

 facebook.com/AuthorNicoleFalls

 twitter.com/_nicolefalls

 instagram.com

Made in the USA
Middletown, DE
10 September 2023